THE DEMON OF THE ABSURD

"RACHILDE" was the pen name of Marguerite Vallette-Eymery (1860–1953), one of the most important writers of the Decadent Movement. Her works include the novels *Monsieur Vénus* (1884), and *The Princess of Darkness* (1895), the latter book being written under the pseudonym Jean de Chilra. She also wrote a 1928 monograph on gender identity, *Pourquoi je ne suis pas féministe* ("Why I am not a Feminist").

MARCEL SCHWOB (1867-1905) was sent to Paris in 1881 to study at the Lycée Louis-le-Grand, where he met the future writers Léon Daudet and Paul Claudel; he lived with his uncle, the novelist Léon Cahun. He became a professional journalist in 1888, working on both *L'Événement* and *L'Écho de Paris*.

SHAWN GARRETT is a freelance editor, critic and short fiction aficionado. He currently co-edits the horror fiction podcast *Pseudopod* and posts weekly columns with *Rue Morgue*. His translations include Robert Scheffer's *Prince Narcissus and Other Stories* (Snuggly Books, 2019), and Gabriel Mourey's *Monada* (Snuggly Books, 2021).

RACHILDE

THE DEMON OF THE ABSURD

TRANSLATED BY
SHAWN GARRETT

&

WITH A PREFACE BY
MARCEL SCHWOB

THIS IS A SNUGGLY BOOK

Translation Copyright © 2024
by Shawn Garrett.
All rights reserved.

ISBN: 978-1-64525-151-4

This book is dedicated to my younger sister, Jennifer Pinkasavage, a fine photographer, loving wife and caring human being. I hope she knows how proud I am of her, as she holds an important position at the Disney Corporation, and how much gratitude I have towards her for taking on the responsibility of caring for our mother.

—*Shawn Garrett*

CONTENTS

Preface / *9*

Smoke / *17*
The Crystal Spider / *23*
The Hermetic Chateau / *37*
The Unholy Parade / *51*
The Harvest of Sodom / *63*
The Prowler / *73*
The Tooth / *83*
Pleasure / *91*
The Ghost Trap / *103*
A Bother / *117*
The Panther / *127*
Universal Joy / *135*
The Hands / *137*

PREFACE

*Credibile est quia ineptum est...
certum est quia impossible.*
Tertullianus. *De carne Christi*, 5.

"IT is a good bet," says Chamfort, quoted by Edgar Poe, "that any public idea, any accepted convention, is a folly, because it is agreed upon by the largest number."

I wouldn't want to define the absurd any other way. Between the opinion of a single man and the opinion of the multitude, one cannot hesitate. We read in the *Gospel of Saint Luke*[1] that the demons who called themselves "Legion" prayed to Jesus to allow them to enter the body of the wandering pigs on the mountain. Jesus permitted them, and the possessed swine rushed to the precipice. Thus the demon of the absurd entered the body of the legion;

---

1 see F. Dostoyevsky: *The Possessed*

and the multitude rushes towards its precipice, making its laws and obeying its conventions—for such are the commandments of the foolish demon.

It is therefore not in this book that you will find the demon of the absurd; but exercising its power of terror, it roams all around, as the prowler in a short story you are about to read roams the house. Beware of fleeing into the black countryside: for the prowling demon will seize you. But in the kitchen of the house leave the candle which continues to burn, resembling a funeral taper; and sit there in the pen. Do not leave the pages of this book, for you will be harassed by swine possessed of foolishness and, outside, the Devil prowls in his kingdom of dark absurdity.

There is no other reality than things invented by an inimitable imagination. Everything else is foolishness or error. "The truly strong man is the man who is alone." If Rachilde is the only one to be frightened by mirrors, to contemplate in the glory of the sunset or the hermetic castle where she will never enter, to experience the pangs of death for a pulled tooth, it is because she sees further than we. The master of the absurd has entered our bodies, according to Jesus' permission, and our sight has become obscured. If Rachilde's tales seem absurd to the demon named "Legion," we can be sure that they contain an invaluable part of the truth.

All things are related. When we grasp their positional relations, we classify them according to cause and effect. When we conceive them according to their relations of resemblance and magnitude, we classify them according to the logical ideas of our mind. These notions being common to all philosophers, it is a safe bet that they are not sufficient for the truth. One can imagine that things have other relationships between them than the scientific and the logical. They can relate to each other as signs. For signs have no absolute quantity or quality. And it is possible that the signs being very different, the things signified are very similar. Of these signified things neither the senses nor the intelligence can know anything. But the dogs that howl at death don't know it's coming. Thus Rachilde when she cries out in terror resembles Cassandra screaming to death in front of the black porch of the Atrides. Cassandra doesn't know what will terrify her. Rachilde is unaware of the tragic relationship of the things that haunt her. But she senses them and a sacred trepidation seizes her.

See the little woman who has lost a tooth. "Oh, she felt when that fell between the pieces of the croquet, like a little cold heart was escaping from her. She has just expired entirely in a tiny detail of her person."

And the two old women whom Rachilde knew, and who died saying: "We are not at home here! This is not where we should die."

Can you deduce the effect from the cause, formulate the main reasoning that leads to this conclusion? Yet there is a deep connection between the lost tooth and total corruption; and the dying old women sense more than language can express. It is the same obscure power of union which brings death to the end of voluptuousness, which evokes the obscenity of small fat hands, which blurs with sadness the spring landscape with its branches of almond trees in blossom. Everywhere Cassandra shudders and senses the inexplicable. For it has been given to her to experience the mysterious relations of signs. It has been said that women have antennae in their hearts. Rachilde has an antennae in her brain. To have guessed by the age of twenty, in writing *"A Bother"(La Scie)*, the irremediable mediocrity of life and its uselessness, one needs an intellectual hyperesthesia that feminine sensibility alone cannot explain. With these delicate filaments that extend her intelligence, she scents death through love, the obscene through health, terror through calm and silence. Like a listening cat, she pricks up her ears, and she hears the little mouse of death which gnaws, gnaws at the walls, the ideas, the flesh. And she voluptuously extends her paw to play with the deadly little mouse.

—Marcel Schwob

THE DEMON OF THE ABSURD

THE SMOKE

For Pierre Guillard

(Transcription of handwritten pages.)

THE smoke rises madly towards the clarity of the blue heavens. They go to war, the smoke against the implacable azure.

Oh! The furious smoke, the desperate smoke, the evil smoke, the useless smoke, the sick smoke, the humble smoke.

❦

The long, taut muzzles of the factories launch black swirls streaked with red sparks, crepe heavy with mourning tears of blood, and the dreadful spirals rise, rise to attack the young ether, that divine ether, eternally radiant. It rushes into the void, the furious smoke, spread out to smear, folded up to smear more deeply, condensing to generate thunderbolts. It unfurls its dark banner of cities crushed by toil, it howls, it writhes, it seeks the stars to steal them like the fierce poor steal gold coins... And the sun, in the morning, devours it little by little, dissolves it, tears it with his mocking rays. It becomes sad mists; the light cloud which flees the dawn goes away, it doesn't matter where, to cry on an unknown mountain all the miseries of which it is full...

Here it is leaving the battlefield, the desperate smoke, made of acrid scents of gunpowder, white, with scarlet reflections and then of a sinister violet, swinging its hot plumes from the tops of the trembling trees. There it is, quick, angry, rising, rising, carrying cries of victory or terror. Sometimes it is all yellow as it passes under the sun, looking like stretched flesh, like a thick flag carved out of livid meat, spattered with shards of bronze...

And the sun, in the evening, takes the desperate fumes, the red fumes, to be haloed by them at sunset!

It rises slowly from the unhealthy swamps, the evil and sly fumes. In its turn, during the times of renewal and the warm twilights, it rises in suffocating vapors, carrying the fever of the earth and all the pestilential miasmas, freeing itself from secret rottenness or heaps of cast-off flowers. Is it soft, enveloping, like a woman's fantasy.

It come together softly, then leaves to go and smother, in a caressing embrace, the laughing azure, the mocking sun... And the sun stops halfway, pulverizes it to throw it, in the spring, into handfuls of pollen on the great virgin meadows...

It raises the useless fumes. All, too, they rise, courageous, independent, some tossed about by the caprice of the northern winds, others frail, tenuous but ferocious as the blasphemies of a child. There are the sighs of agony on winter nights. Here and there, a pure white snowflake: the breath of a poet who warms up by blowing onto his chilled fingers. A bluish flake: the smoke of the cigar that the atheist savors. A purple snowflake: the asphyxiation of the abandoned girl, murderous mist flying out of the window, broken too late! Oh! The useless fumes! Above all, above all, the useless fumes of incense! They rise, they rise... And the haughty sun makes the tears of the rebels, the sobs of prayers, the tears of love, ooze onto the accursed cities, in a cold mist...

◆

Like a diaphanous cloud, it rises through the wide chimneys of the hospices, the pale sick smoke, and the coughing fits of the chest-beaters, the boiling herbal teas, the short breaths of the operated upon, rise, rise painfully, dragging themselves, narrating, bearing witness to the unheard-of torture endured by the unfortunates punished for having wanted to live.

Oh! The desolate smoke! And, indifferent, the sun sprinkles with it, the autumn, the asphalt of our boulevards: it is the lugubrious rain of November, which knocks down the leaves, a valetudinary rain...

◆

It did not rise for the young ether, that humble smoke! It fell on the fresh roses in dew, the exhalations of withered roses. And the last little breaths that the old little birds have sown, on the moss, bitter droplets that the sun has drunk without seeing them!

The smoke rises like mad towards the clarity of the blue heavens; it returns to war, the smoke, to war against an implacable azure!

THE CRYSTAL SPIDER

For Jules Renard

A large living room including one of the three windows open onto a terrace filled with honeysuckle. Very clear summer night. The moon illuminates the entire part where the characters are. The background remains dark. We glimpse furniture, heavy and old-fashioned in appearance. In the center of this semi-darkness, a high Empire-style mirror, held on each side by a long swan's neck with a copper beak. A vague reflection of light on the mirror, but, seen from the lit terrace, this reflection does not seem to come from the moon, it seems to come out of the very psyche like a light of its own.

The Mother: *45 years old, lively eyes, tender mouth; it is a young figure under gray hair. She wears an elegant black housecoat and a white lace mantilla. Sensual voice.*

The Frightened: *20 years old. He is thin, and seems as if floating in his outfit of pure white canvas. His face is earthy, his eyes are fixed. His straight black hair glistens on his forehead. He has regular features reminiscent of his mother's beauty, much as a dead man might look like in her portrait. Voice muffled and slow.*

The two figures are seated in front of the open door.

THE MOTHER: Come now, my little son, what are you thinking?

THE FRIGHTENED: But... nothing, mother.

THE MOTHER (*reclining in her armchair*): What a perfume, this honeysuckle! Do you feel it intoxicate you? It smells like one of those fine lady's liqueurs... (*she clicks her tongue.*)

THE FRIGHTENED: A liqueur, this honeysuckle? Ah... yes, mother.

THE MOTHER: You're not cold, I hope, from this weather? And you don't have a migraine?

THE FRIGHTENED: No, thank you, mother.

THE MOTHER: Thank you, what? (*she bends down and looks at him attentively.*) My poor little Sylvius! Admit it, it's not fun to keep an old woman company. (*Sniffing the breeze*) What a sweet night! It's useless to ask for the lamps, isn't it? I told François to go for a walk, and I bet he chases the maids' skirts. We'll stay here until the moon wanes... (*Moment of silence. She resumes gravely*) Sylvius, no matter how hard you try to deny it, you're heartbroken. The more you continue, the more you lose weight...

THE FRIGHTENED: I have already declared to you, mother, that I love no one but you.

THE MOTHER (*tenderly*): This is nonsense! Let's see, if she's a princess's daughter, we could afford her anyway. And if she's a vulgar servant, as long as you don't marry her...

THE FRIGHTENED: Mother, your teasing is driving needles into my eardrum.

THE MOTHER: And if there's a debt, a big debt, huh? You know I can pay it.

THE FRIGHTENED: No debt! I have more money than I can spend.

THE MOTHER (*lowering her voice and drawing her chair closer*): So... you're not going to be angry, Sylvius? By the lady, you men, you have more shameful secrets than bad passions and debts. I have resolved to meddle in everything... do you hear me? If one who is my own flesh were ill... well (*finely*), we would heal ourselves...

THE FRIGHTENED (*with a gesture of disgust*): You are mad, mother.

THE MOTHER (*with outburst*): Yes, I am indeed beginning to believe that I am losing my mind just looking at you! (*She gets up.*) Don't you realize that you frighten me?

THE FRIGHTENED (*starting*): Fear!

THE MOTHER (*returning and leaning over him, coaxing*): I didn't want to upset you, my Sylvius! (*Pause, then she gets up, and speaks vehemently*) Oh! who is the beggar who took my Sylvius? Because there is a beggar, that's for sure...

THE FRIGHTENED (*shrugging his shoulders*): I can suggest several, if that suits you, my mother.

THE MOTHER (*remaining standing and seeming to be talking to herself*): Or else a dreadful vice, one of those vices which we honest women do not even suspect. (*She speaks to him.*) Since you've been like this, I've been reading novels to try to understand you, and I haven't yet discovered anything that I don't already know.

THE FRIGHTENED: Oh! I suspect so.

THE MOTHER: It's decided! Tomorrow, we will invite women, young girls. You will see Sylvia, your cousin. You used to follow her like a doggie, and she has become charming; a bit flirtatious, for example, but so curious with her imitations of all the singers in vogue! Oh! my darling, the woman must be the only concern of the man. Then love makes you beautiful! (*She strokes his chin.*) You can ask for the mirror in your bathroom again!

THE FRIGHTENED(*drawing up with a gesture of horror*): The mirror in my bathroom! My God! women, young girls, creatures who all have mirror reflections deep in their eyes. Mother! You want to kill me...

THE MOTHER (*surprised*): What! More ideas about mirrors! So it's serious, this mania? My word, he ended up thinking he was ugly. (*She laughs.*)

THE FRIGHTENED (*casting a furtive glance behind him, towards the side of the psyche that the moon illuminates in the distance*): Mom, please, let's abandon this discussion. No, my physique is not at stake. There are moral causes. My God! Can you see that I am suffocating! Will you understand! Oh, for eight days, this has been an incessant persecution! You overwhelm me! No, I'm not ill! I need solitude, that's all. Invite all the mirrors you like, and hang all the women of the earth on the wall, but don't tickle me to make me laugh. Ah! It's too much, it's too much!... (*He falls back in his armchair.*)

THE MOTHER (*encircling him with her arms*): You're suffocating, Sylvius, but who is doing it? Me, I'm dying of grief to see you with that taciturn face. You need to leave to be happy, I am able to understand you, go... since I adore you! (*She kisses him.*)

THE FRIGHTENED (*explosively*): Well! Yes, there, I'm afraid of mirrors, have me locked up if you want!
(*Moment of silence.*)

THE MOTHER (*gently*): We'll lock up the mirrors, Sylvius.

THE FRIGHTENED (*holding out his hands to her*): Forgive me, mother, I am brutal. No doubt I should have spoken sooner, but it is agony to think that people are going to make fun of you. And that can hardly be said in two words... (*He passes his hands over his forehead*) Mother, what do you see when you look at yourself? (He breathes with difficulty.)

THE MOTHER: I see myself, my Sylvius (*She sits down sadly and shakes her head*), I see an old woman! Alas!

THE FRIGHTENED (*throwing her a look of commiseration*): Ah! Have you never seen anyone *in there* but yourself? I pity you! (*becoming animated*) And me, it seems to me that the inventor of the first mirror must have gone mad with terror in the presence of his work! So, for you, a smart woman, there are only simple things in a mirror? In this atmosphere of the unknown, do you not see an army of ghosts suddenly rise? On the threshold of these gates to dream, you have not unraveled a spell of infinity which was watching you? But it's so frightening, a mirror, that I'm bewildered, every morning, to know I am alive, but you, the women and young girls are all constantly gazing at me! Mother, listen to me, this is all a story, and you have to go back a long way to discover the cause of my hatred for reflecting glass, because I am predestined, I was *warned* in my childhood... I was ten years old, I was over there, in the pavilion in our park, all alone, and in the presence of a big, big mirror that hasn't been there for a long time. I was leafing through my school notebooks, I had a syllabus to write. That closed room, with the drawn curtains, struck me as a poor man's house, furnished with garden chairs all eaten away with damp, a table covered with a dirty carpet with holes in it. The ceiling was dripping, you could hear the rain pounding on a half-demolished zinc roof. The only idea of luxury was created by this large mirror, oh! so tall, as tall as a person! Mechanically, I looked at myself. Beneath the limpidity of the glass there were gloomy stains. One would have said that water lilies, rounded on the surface of a still water, and further away, in the depths of darkness, stood indecisive forms which resembled specters moving through the stream with their muddy hair. I remember that, while admiring myself, I had the strange sensation of stepping up to my neck in this ice as in a silty lake. I had been locked up, I was on penance, and so I had to, willy-nilly, remain in this dead water. By dint of fixing my eyes on the eyes of my image, I distinguished a brilliant point in the middle of these mists, and at the same time I perceived a slight insect noise coming from the place where I saw the point. Very imperceptibly this point irradiated like a star. It sparkled like a living fulguration within this atmosphere of sleep, it rustled like a fly against a pane of glass. Mother! I saw and I heard that! I wasn't dreaming in the least. No possible explanation for a kid of ten, any more than for a man, I assure you! I knew that the pavilion adjoined a shed where the gardening tools were stored; it was not inhabited. I told myself that probably some spider of an unknown species was going to jump on my face, and, stupidly, I remained there, my arms frozen to my body. The white spider was still advancing, it was becoming a young crab with a silver shell, its head was studded with dazzling ridges, its legs were still stretching out to my reflected head, it was invading my forehead, splitting my temples, devouring my eyes, was gradually erasing my image, beheading me. For a moment I saw myself standing, arms twisted in horror, carrying on my shoulders a monstrous beast that had the sinister appearance of an octopus! I wanted to scream; only, as happens in all nightmares, I couldn't. I now felt at the mercy of the crystal spider, which was sucking my brains out! And it continued to rustle, with the hum of an animal that has the idea of finishing off an enemy once and for all. Fiction crumbled into sparkling crumbs, one of which slightly injured my hand. I uttered heartrending cries and I fainted... When I was able to understand, our gardener, who had entered my prison to reassure me, showed me the crankshaft he was using, on the other side of the wall, for the sole purpose of planting a huge nail! The wall pierced, he had also pierced the glass, suspecting nothing, continuing his work accompanied by the creaking of the tool. My wound was not serious. The good man was afraid of scenes... and I promised to be silent... From that day on, mirrors have singularly preoccupied me, in spite of the nervous aversion I felt for them. My short existence shimmers with their satanic reflections. And after the first physical shock, I received many other spiritual shocks... Here, it's the grotesque memory of the head I had under my college laurels. There, it is the transparent photograph of my libertine sins... There is a mystery in this pursuit of the mirror, in this hunt for a guilty man, directed against me alone! (*He becomes dreamy for a moment, then resumes, becoming more and more animated.*) Against me alone? But no! Believe it, mother, those who see *well* are as terrified as I am. In short, do we know why this piece of glass that we are contemplating suddenly takes on the depths of an abyss... and doubles the world? The mirror is the problem of life, perpetually opposed to man! Do we know exactly what Narcissus saw in the fountain and what he died of?

THE MOTHER (*shuddering*): Oh! Sylvius! You scare me now. Aren't you telling me tall tales? Do you... sincerely think these things?

THE FRIGHTENED: Mother, would you dare, at this hour, go look in a mirror?

THE MOTHER (*turning towards the back living room and very troubled*): No! No! I wouldn't dare... If we lit a lamp...

THE FRIGHTENED (*forcing her to sit down again and sneering*): There... I knew very well that you, too, would be afraid! Presently, you will see it very clearly! Why do you persist, woman, in populating our apartments with these cynical errors which mean that

I can never, *never* be alone? Why are you throwing this spy-man at my head, who has the ability to cry my tears? I saw, one evening when I was putting a fur coat on your shoulders on leaving a ball, I saw in a mirror smiling voluptuously a lady who looked like you, my mother! One morning when I was waiting for my cousin Sylvia, languishing behind her door, a bouquet of orchids in my hand, I saw this door half open on an immense mirror in which was reflected a beautiful naked girl in a provocative pose! Mirrors, mother, are abysses where both the virtue of women and the tranquility of men sink.

THE MOTHER: Be quiet! I don't want to listen to you anymore.

THE FRIGHTENED (*grabbing her arm and rising*): Mother, have you seen the reflecting glasses that catch you as you pass in the streets of big cities? The ones that fall on you suddenly like showers? The mirrors of the storefronts surrounded by odiously fake frames, like the makeup and rhinestones of creatures for sale? Have you seen them offer you their radiant flanks where all the passers-by have successively serviced them? These infernal mirrors! They harass us from all sides! They arise from oceans, rivers, streams! Drinking from my glass, I notice my hideousness. The neighbor who thinks he only has one ulcer always has two! Mirrors are denunciation personified, and they transform a simple inconvenience into an infinite despair. They are in the drop of dew to make the heart of a flower a heart swollen with sobs. Alternately full of lying promises of joy or filled with shameful secrets (and sterile like prostitutes), they keep neither an imprint nor a color. If, in front of the mirror that I am contemplating, *she* has slipped into the arms of *another*, it is always me whom I see in place of *the other*! (*Furious*) They are scandalous torturers who remain impassive, and yet, endowed with the power of Satan. And if they saw God, my mother, they would be like him!

THE MOTHER (*pleading*): Sylvius! The moon is at the angle of the wall. Go get a lamp, I want to see...

THE FRIGHTENED (*in a voice that has become deaf again*): Oh! I tell you these things because you force me to! I really have no ability to become the fatal revealer, but it is good that blind women appreciate, by chance, the appalling situation they create for men who see, even in darkness. You lavishly install these pitiless jailers in our house, we must put up with them for love of you. And in exchange for our patience they blast us with our image, our villainies, our absurd gestures. Ah, may they be cursed at least once, our doubles! Curse them, our rivals! There is a diabolical pact between them and you. (*In a desolate tone of voice*) Have you noticed, on some snowy winter morning, those birds circling above the trap which sparkles and makes them believe in a miraculous heap of silver oats or golden wheat? Have you seen them, as they fall, fall, one by one, from the heights of the heavens, their bruised wings, their bloody beaks, their eyes still dazzled by the splendors of their chimera! There is the mirror for larks and there is the mirror for men, the one who is on the lookout for the dangerous detour of their dark existence, that one will see themselves die with their foreheads glued to the frozen crystal of its enigma...

The Mother (*clinging to him*): No! Enough! I suffer too much! Your voice is killing me! Anguish is squeezing my throat. Don't you pity your mother, Sylvius? I wanted to know, I was wrong. I am sorry! Go get the lamps, I beg you! (*She gets down on her knees, joins her hands.*) I'm as if paralyzed...

The Frightened (*staggering*): I'm afraid, I... the mirror hidden in the shadows, your great psyche, my mother...

THE MOTHER (*exasperated*): Coward! Am I not even more afraid than you! Will you obey me, in the end!

THE FRIGHTENED (*straightening up, beside himself*): Well, so be it! I'll get you the light! (*He rushes with rage in the direction of the psyche, behind which is the door of the living room. For a moment, he runs in the middle of a deep night... Suddenly, there is the terrible jostling of an enormous piece of furniture, the sonorous noise of a crystal breaking and the lamentable howl of a man with his throat slit...*)

THE HERMETIC CHATEAU

For Marcel Schwob

I knew two old women who died saying, "We're not at *home here*! We shouldn't die *here*." One was a peasant woman from Limousin, very poor, a little mad, whose main obsession consisted in an eternal need for locomotion. She dreamed of a place where she would have been *better*, where she should have *always* lived, and since she did not know this place (which, moreover, she did not even know if it existed anywhere but inside her skull) she repeatedly ejaculated: "Oh! they are very unhappy, those who have no country!" She expired, making a stubborn gesture, signifying: "*Over there!*"

The other, a Countess of Beaumont-Landry, had all her reason but she thought for whole days of the *house of her dreams*, and this house did not represent, for her, a sentimental phrase from her youth: it was *really, sincerely*, a house built somewhere, perhaps in Sweden or in Ireland, in a country *the color of gray lace*, she said, *where doves must be in mourning*. She defined nothing, wished for nothing. Neither paintings nor engravings gave her more precise indications, but she knew that this house was *over there*, and that her position as a pampered socialite, was noted in this modest place of rest. When she was in agony, she took her daughter's hands, whispered to her in a very worried voice: "I am not *here* at home! No, this is not *here* where I should be, nor the *brother country*, without which one does not live happily, and so how can one obtain a peaceful end?"

How many melancholic tourists have said with regret in their eyes: "I saw the place I would like to live in passing, and I no longer remember in which corner of the earth it is! I no longer know the name of the village... I no longer see the shade of the sky..."

How many famous explorers have felt suddenly drawn, across seas and deserts, towards a mysterious site, a homeland made for them alone, of which they possess within them an image so erased that it seems to them to be the memory of an old print admired too long during their childhood!

And there are the cursed places where we

go because we have to go there, where we encounter the wound that has been destined to us for centuries. There is the forest that haunts you, from afar, and where you hang from the tree that you believe you have already seen elsewhere, a tree that held out its branches to you behind all the twilight windows. There is the lost lake at the bottom of the little wild valley, the greenish pool bristling with black brush, into which one throws oneself with the almost joy of having finally found one's own grave, and a grave in no way similar to that of your neighbor. For all eternity the places for our feet have probably been designated, but they do not come to light according to our will: our parents are agitated, move away, go, come uselessly, themselves seek their definitive residence, so that it takes multiple tries to inform us, to provide us with solemn intuition and to lift us, as if on wings, to the country which guards, in a field of wheat or in a deserted street, the mystical roots of our person.

Often, too, in ecstasy before this countryside, we see it suddenly recede, melt away, vanish. It flees from us, abandons us, and for a reason that will never be given to us, because, no doubt, *it is too frightening*, we guess that we will not reach it, that this promised land will be eternally stolen from us.

And here is what I want to say *very sincerely*, about one of these countries of chimeras, which I *really* found in my travels:

It was in Franche-Comté, while visiting on a beautiful sunny day a large sad property located near the village of Roquemont, in the small hamlet of Suse. We had climbed the summit of a hill which those nearby called *Dent de l'Ours*, because of its strange indentation, and the three of us were lying on red grass which smelled of burnt hair. The mother, Madame Téard, the son, Albert Téard, and I were all very hot; we talked no more, having exhausted all the banal Parisian stories. At this height, on this plateau swept by the dry breezes, the source of vulgar conversations had suddenly dried up within us, and we only wanted to stifle the echoes of the towns, always so explosive in the religious silence as of a rise of Calvary. My friends had first graciously insisted on having me judge the house, the garden, the vineyard; from different sides, they pointed out to me the celebrities of the country: the place where last year Albert Téard had killed an enormous hare, the crossroads where the remains of Prussians could still be seen, the path down which from the wood descended, on certain winters, the thieving wolves. Then, little by little, seized with a respect for the enveloping grandeur of the panorama, we fell silent without consulting each other, and we looked almost without seeing.

On the horizon, though not too far away, stood an enormous rock on another hill, sister to the one that carried us, and you could very distinctly see the ruins of a feudal castle forming as one body with the dark rock. This made a dramatic backdrop to the relatively gay picture represented by the village of Susa, huddled against a naive rounded belfry, and the vineyard, where peasants in blouses and women in light skirts were scattered. It towered over the town with an evil, imperious air, and it was impossible not to declare at once that there was a truly *curious* place, a point of history or legend. But we hadn't talked about it yet. Albert Téard, in a doleful tone, murmured:

"...There are also caverns full of fossil bones and carved flints; we'll get you there; then you will have seen everything."

"How can I have seen everything? I said, raising myself on one elbow; "but not the ruins over there?"

"Huh? What ruins?" asked Madame Téard, astonished.

My eyes were fixed. I stretched out my arm, and Albert Téard began to laugh.

"Those, ruins? Maybe so, and more likely than not! From our house, on a rainy day, it just looks like sheer rock, but, in the sun with plays of light falling from the clouds, it sometimes *seems* like an old castle without a door. Oh! don't believe it!"

"Are you kidding?" I stared, fascinated, my brain hurting.

"No, it's the rock which is joking," continued Albert Téard. "There is no description of these ruins in the annals of Franche-Comté, and our peasants, who have no time to amuse themselves, claim never to have distinguished them, neither in the sun nor in the rain. As for me, I no longer see them except vaguely... *because I have known for a long time what to expect.*"

"As for me," said Madame Téard softly, "an exquisite, reasonable old woman, I have often tried to picture the château for myself, and I have not been able to discover the slightest turret!"

I was stunned. From instant to instant the mirage became more accentuated, became formidable; I saw braces, warheads, crenellations, and all these bluish details darkened as if under the strokes of a fantastic brush. Téard's mother smiled, leaning her good face on her left shoulder.

"So you want to risk the bad rascal's leap?"

"What is the 'bad rascal?' A legend?"

"No, a very natural adventure. He was a conscript who had bet on finding buzzard eggs up there before going to the regiment, and, as it was gray the morning he attempted his ascent, he tumbled from your famous castle to his cottage. If he didn't find buzzard eggs, he certainly found a police cell when he arrived at his captain's, because he had to be treated and he missed the first call, that simpleton."

I remained in contemplation in front of the magic castle. A mist surrounded the hill, covered with tall junipers and thickets of beech trees. One dreamed there of the coolness of water hidden in the depths *of the dungeons*, and the rock, at a distance, seemed to shine like the skin of a reptile. A foot from the first body of the building, a kind of bulge cut in a walkway looked exactly like human work, and it seemed so easy to walk on it that I couldn't understand the disdain of my friends.

"We will go! It's understood," decided Téard with a sardonic grimace.

We went there the next day. Madame Téard followed us, carrying a copiously filled basket, because, she said, "*it is always further than we thought.*"

After an hour's walk in the wheat and in the vineyards, we arrived on the stony slope of a hill. Dug in its center, mourning in its thick and cold shadow, was a hamlet of five or six poor hovels. Here and there, taciturn people. The men were arranging barrels without shouting or swearing. The women, cradling infants, did not sing. Perhaps it was just me, all by myself, that had this special vision of a sleeping village, since my companions didn't really notice anything abnormal while crossing this corner of the shady country. However, Madame Téard, having wanted to buy a little milk, noticed that no one was even answering her, and she said to me in a bored voice:

"They are like that here!"

The old lady settled down on the edge of a primitive wash-house where a fountain gurgled through wooden pipes. She wished us a happy climb and began to plunge bottles into the water for the return trip. In vain did I tell myself that this was now a question of a pleasant excursion, not the conquest I was completely desperate to advance. I could no longer distinguish the feudal rock behind the ordinary rocks, which hid it from me. The silence of the hamlet gripped me, I was nervous. This romantic mirage of the day before was turning into a ridiculous ambush, and I vibrated as if I were already the victim of a terrible injustice. Téard, philosophically, pointed out to me that our leggings were solid, begged me to arm myself with patience because of the inextricable brambles that we would have to cross:

"But you demanded it!" he stated.

To move in a straight line towards the *château* seemed to me a mere childish attack; but, minute by minute, it became a very serious battle plan. We deviated, in spite of ourselves. We retreated before the ditches filled with mire, thorns, and sharp stones. We were forced to turn around for difficulties, got tangled up in each other, and we ended up turning our backs on our goal. Curtains of rosehips and brambles, brushwood tall enough to lay on the ground, further hid the ruins from us, and when a clearing under the branches let us see them, the eye struck an enormous wall, a plain wall. The dungeons, the crenellations, the walkway, had been completely swallowed up in this oozing damp wall, and there remained standing only a mute, blind facade, the threatening facade par excellence, the hermetic facade. We sat down halfway up, all out of breath, on a tree trunk.

"Eh?" said Téard to me, wiping his forehead, "it's annoying!"

"We have to find a shortcut as soon as possible, I want to touch this rock with both hands."

Here we went again, the nose up, eyes worried. Téard was seized with a fever, and he confessed to me that we didn't really know the end of this damned rock. In the past, quarries could well have been dug in the hill, perhaps they had tried to build something in the rock itself, and, no doubt, they had given up trying in the presence of the hardness of the granite. Only, if there was *something*, how did we reach the top of the edifice? How had they crossed this front of the wall, so smooth that it gleamed?

"With ladders?"

"Let's get on with it! This is that conscript's adventure! This boy had dragged knotted ropes and crampons. He erected ladders, sometimes to the east, sometimes to the west; you could see him from below struggling like the devil, and he was no more drunk than I am. Nevertheless, it ended in a mad tumble. A dip into the fountain, head first! No! We may need a balloon!"

When we were at the foundations of the *château*, our nostrils inhaled the acrid perfume of the green moss which velveted them, we were much less advanced than halfway up; we no longer grasped anything of the whole, and the details led our imaginations astray in the midst of the most stupid conjectures.

"Let's circumvent!" I exclaimed.

One veered west, the other east. We were to meet under what I called the walkway. To walk, I hung on shrubs, clumps of grass, the ground was extremely slippery and stones fell between my legs, went rolling down to the fountain where our picnic wine was refreshing. One could hear the rocks leaping from ditch to ditch, hitting outcrops and then falling in the foliage like dead birds. The earth was crumbling under my feet, oddly friable, flowing in heavy streams, full of a quantity of shiny brown flakes perhaps resembling the scales of a gigantic antediluvian fish. The greasy greenery left a sticky sap on your hand, and you breathed, very close to the moss, a smell of rottenness. When I raised my head, I found the imposing line of this monument without door or window, and my gaze, soaring desperately, could cling neither to an asperity of the stone, nor to a small flower. The rock, always the rock, shiny, oozing, without a crack, without a hole. And up there, very high, in the light, hovered the silver-winged buzzards, slowly, like calm swimmers who abandon themselves to the gentle waves of a blue ocean. There are hours when the pure air intoxicates you, makes you forget the *down to earth* of things. For a second, it seemed almost simpler to me to have a balloon!

Oh! To enter the castle which I had seen, and which *existed* since *I had seen it*! Penetrate inside the mysterious citadel, where it seemed to me *decidedly* that someone was waiting for me! Yes, I must arrive there one day! I had to touch the colossal wall with my poor helpless hands, bang my forehead against the granite to summon the people I needed to free! And I listened, I scrutinized the inexorable hardness of this natural pyramid to try to glean some note of recognition!

All wild sites give you hallucinations and instantaneous monomanias of sizes. When you are alone on a mountain, nothing prevents you from believing that you are king! I could have brushed the top of a Poplar with my legging, and at the very bottom I saw Madame Téard sleeping under her white parasol lined with red, Madame Téard as big as a ladybug with a pink head! Well, then? Why wasn't the drawbridge lowered? Finally, dizziness overtook me, and with my eyes furiously closed, I started to circumvent again.

Beneath the walkway, Téard was examining a trace in the stone. This excited us for a moment. It looked like the mark of an iron ring, one of those rings that are planted on quays to moor ships. For a good quarter of an hour we stayed there, clinging to the strength of our nails above the abyss, studying this weak vestige of humanity, and we had to conclude that a pebble, coming out of its sandstone cell like a stone sticks out of a ripe fruit, had probably formed this ring mark. We had to go back down. We walked away, each one very absorbed, with the unhappy faces of individuals who were turned away because we weren't well enough dressed. All the way down we had terrible accidents, I fell into a ditch full of thorns, and Téard stepped on a viper. At the bottom, Madame Téard, awake, was watching us, her face confused, her arms in the air: a stray dog had robbed the basket of provisions; the wine, too shaken by the eddies of the fountain, was wasted. We had some bread left, but a bread that had already been eaten away, covered in drool. Téard, disappointed, laughed furiously. His mother lamented. I dared not say anything more. The sun was setting; we went home quickly for dinner.

During the meal, as the window was open on a marvelous horizon of flames and gold, I uttered a real cry of anger, pointing to them with my index finger the distant hill. Over there... over there, a diabolical play of purple lights, purple shadows, made the ruins of the feudal castle reappear. I distinguished more clearly than ever the dungeons, the walkway, the battlements; and, more formidably than ever, rose up, in the blood of the dying day, the *Hermetic Castle*, the unknown fatherland which drew my heart!

THE UNHOLY PARADE

For Remy De Gourmont

SCENERY: At night, in a church.
Characters: Rhymes of things and Reasons of people.

The Moon (*entering through a stained glass window*): How dark it is in this well!

The Bell Tower (*with resignation*): She takes me for a well! If that's how history is to be written here...

The Moon (*an indifferent citizen*): And there are huge cobwebs.

The Stained Glass Saint (*waking up without his shroud of dust*): Oh! Who's there! I saw a blonde go by. She entwined her hair with my nimbus. These creatures respect nothing. Fortunately, I'm made of glass today, and less fragile than before. (*He yawns.*)

THE LAST CHING OF THE BAPTISM BELL: Later, *they* will understand the melancholy of these joyous tunes.

THE LAST CHING OF THE BURIAL BELL: The good feast, as the ringer drank!

FIRST BAT (*swirling*): Heaven and earth! I'm only a poor bird, but all that seems very ridiculous to me.

SECOND BAT (*circling*): Earth and sky! I'm only a poor mouse, but all this bothers me.

THE LARGE CANDLE ON THE RIGHT: My wax has the whiteness of beautiful brides.

THE LARGE CANDLE ON THE LEFT: My wax has the whiteness of pretty children, dead.

A CANDLE IN A CORNER: Mine has the purity of stearin, a chemical virtue.

FIRST NIGHT-LAMP: I am a woman's heart filled with pink rubies.

SECOND NIGHT-LAMP: I am the eye of a lover who cries a lot.

THE DEAD UNDER A SLAB: Help! Get me out of here! I'm suffocating! Remove the stone, because my nails grow into roots and lengthen without finding any crack. Remove the stone!

THE DEAD UNDER ANOTHER SLAB: Why haven't they planted me at the edge of a stream? I carry in my eyes two seeds of forget-me-nots.

A Confessional: I am a supply of darkness locked in a closet.

The Trunk for the Poor: They filled me with bronze washers, silver washers, gold washers; but, in the midst of these vulgar coins, shines a marvelous piece, unique no doubt. It is pierced with four small holes and adorned, in highlights, with mysterious words. Ah! the one who gave it was a truly charitable man. I would like to know him.

A Prayer Bench: His knees are very light. Her dress smelled good, and I have strands of silk among my strands of straw.

A Chair: Oh! The rotundities of old women!

A Carpet: A lily petal, still fresh, was stuck to her heel and I knew it came from her father's garden.

The Altar Steps: This is outrageous! The priest never looks where he steps before entering the church.

Chorus of Organ Pipes: *Dies iræ! Te Deum! Alleluia! De profundis!*

A Swallow (*leaning from the top of the rose window*): I think the weather will be fine tomorrow!

An Echo: Amen!

(*Silence.*)

(*A padded door opens slowly and falls back with a thud. Enter* The Cursed, The

Prostitute *and* The Jew, *groping their way*.)

The Cursed (*staggering a little and bending down to light a lantern*): Eh! See, I told you! Nobody! Those places are always empty, at night... humanity only cares about God when they can't make love. (*He shakes his rags, laughing sadly.*)

The Prostitute (*in an annoyed tone, tightening her mourning shawl over her red satin dress*): Shut up! Now is not the time to joke. Me, I hate houses whose ceilings are... ahh, to hell with it!

The Jew (*taking off his rabbit skin cap*): We always owe respect, that doesn't commit you to anything.

The Cursed (*in a heartbroken voice*): You are filthy animals, and yet you are safer than I here: you do not believe.

(*All three walk to the altar and* The Cursed *places the lantern on the chancel balustrade.*)

The Prostitute (*supporting* The Cursed *who is staggering*): Let's talk a little, let's talk well; you promised us extraordinary jewels: where are they?

The Cursed (*stretching out his arm with a stiff gesture, and pointing to the tabernacle*): They are there.

The Jew (*shaking his head*): It is understood that you will fetch them alone...

THE PROSTITUTE: On his own, since the idea came from him. Me, I would never have thought of such a farce.

THE JEW (*mocking*): Me neither, it's a brilliant idea, and so simple!

THE CURSED (*tortured*): So, if it's so simple, go ahead.

THE JEW (*pulling out a scale, weights, iron tongs from under his coat*): Lender, buyer, be I. A thief, no! I come above all to please Madame.

AN ECHO: Lady!

THE PROSTITUTE (*furious*): Would my lover be a chicken!

THE CURSED (*raising his head proudly*): What chicken would dare measure himself against God? Yes, I want to steal it; only, I also want to battle it. This is the fortress I will loyally rob only after having explained my reasons. I'll talk really loud, even if you bullies don't listen.

(*He leaps and jumps into the choir over the balustrade. Mechanically* THE PROSTITUTE *kneels down, while* THE JEW *examines the beam of his scales.* THE CURSED *continues in a serious tone, addressing the tabernacle.*)

My God, I am the prey brought to you by beasts of prey; but, as a gallant man who wishes to equalize the chances of this fabulous duel, I will count my grievances. For your part, prepare your thunderbolts, I will not violate you in full sleep. Oh! My life is bare, King of Kings! If you don't remember my miseries, I bring them to you. Judge! Cursed by my carnal father, abandoned by my mother, I rolled from abyss to abyss. I've killed, I've cheated at gambling and I've lied. You let me walk up to you the better to annihilate me, I think, and here comes the hour of the supreme fall, of sin without remission, of sacrilege. I don't hesitate, I try to justify myself. Aren't you more guilty than me, you, God whose right hand is too immobile, and can't you spare me as an accomplice or destroy me suddenly? I give you back my paradise, if not snatch my heart from my chest. It's time to make up your mind. I may be the last of the believers. And look behind me at this woman with her red dress, her shoulders pale as snowflakes melting on a bright fire. She needs jewelry, I don't have any. When she waves her little hand, Lord, you who see everything, you must have noticed it, it seems that suddenly the tip of an angel's wing pushes you, and we go madly to the big crime. God, have compassion! What torture will you invent stronger than this contempt! I traveled the roads, I was hungry and I had the urge to graze the flowering grass between the legs of the oxen. At the end of the road, I drank, like the others. I was asked for money and I begged. I even learned to play dog, to crawl, to draw hoarse sounds from my thirsty throat. I bit... then I met this girl who caressed me; my only moment of joy, she holds it in the secret folds of her skirt of flame, and my worst torment is still to have known her! You understand, most intelligent God, I need your diamonds... You have more of them... (*He raises his arms.*)

AN ECHO: More!

THE CURSED: Lord! You must give them to me willingly. You can't. (*Moving.*) And she's a child who can't laugh without a toy. (*He grows impatient.*) My belief in you is my entire fortune. Answer me! The *bourse* or death! Kill the criminal before the crime or enrich him, in the name of faith. (*explosively.*) Ah! if I had thunder at my command...

THE PROSTITUTE (*low to the Jew*): I poured him hot liquors to make him nice. A talkative man always ends up regaining his courage.

THE JEW (*annoyed*): I think we're wasting precious time and I don't much like speeches. (*Reflecting*) After all, churches are full of bones.

THE CURSED (*desperate*): Do you hear me, dead and immortal God, blind and clairvoyant God, God the master and God in chains? I am ready, I approach. Notice that my fingers are bristling like octopuses. I need the sun, gold, stars, pearls, the ocean, emeralds, because my universe is this woman, and I don't have too much of yours to adorn the dark expanse of her hair... (*Silence.*) Nothing! It's enough to break your skull against the door of your prison, an impotent prisoner who allows himself to be insulted, you who remain enclosed in a cup narrower than my mistress's breast. And if you can't deliver yourself, deliver me! (*He sobs.*) Lord, be good! I am weak, I brave you only because I am afraid! Lord, my mother taught me to ask you for daily bread; now, I need to feed this woman, and this woman feeds on jewels! You who intend the sheep for the wolf, give me your finery so that I can buy my daily bread... (*Silence.*)

THE JEW (*sneering*): Never has a drunkard seen himself face to face with such a wall.

THE PROSTITUTE (*with a gesture of boredom*): He doesn't even think that I'm low-class. It's not hot here...

THE CURSED (*approaching the tabernacle and delirious*): All my tears for your precious stones, centuries of hell for a piece of this yellow metal which is useless to you. Lord, alms to the beggar, your servant in sacrilege, that is to say to the one who still believes in you since he takes the trouble to insult you!

THE JEW (*low to the Prostitute*): Did you notice this ciborium? Priests often spread legends...

THE PROSTITUTE (*forcefully*): I came to mass this morning to contemplate it. Oh! stunning! Polished gems all around, and in the center a diamond the size of a dove's egg.

THE JEW: I'm wary of big diamonds. They're usually not fair water.

THE PROSTITUTE: Fair water! You laugh! The only thing pure on earth is a diamond, but your dirty imaginations disturbs everything in advance!

THE JEW (*bowing, mockingly*): The only thing pure on earth is the look of a virgin, Madame.

THE CURSED (*crying*): Woe! Three times misfortune! God wants my damnation! (*He is going to take the iron claw on the railing.*) I am going to force the door of heaven with this! (*He brandishes the pliers and begins to laugh a painful laugh.*) And tomorrow the bankrupt church will have no more hosts to hand through the window of its office. I will rob the treasury of the chosen. (*He knocks on the tabernacle.*) What irony! This door looks like a bank counter. (*He inserts the pliers and makes the wooden blades jump.*) You wanted it, Madelon... And now, lightning strikes!

THE PROSTITUTE (*uttering a cry of joy*): Let it!

THE JEW (*stepping back*): What are you going to do with the hosts? I refuse to concern myself with it.

THE CURSED (*raising the ciborium with a movement of horror*): Empty! It's empty!

THE PROSTITUTE: So much the better! Sometimes they forget to fill it up... and since there's no one in control...

THE CURSED (*rolling his eyes madly*): Nobody, no God, not even a simulacrum of God!

THE JEW: It was to be guessed, since he didn't answer you, my dear boy. Still, let's see the object.

THE CURSED (*letting him take hold of the ciborium*): And the lightning doesn't fall.

THE PROSTITUTE (*shrugging her shoulders*): You are boring us with your perpetual exaggerations.

THE JEW (*turning the ciborium over in the shady gleams of the lantern*): Here! Here! I did not imagine so badly! Oh! Famous legends. (*He bends down, taking on a pitiful air.*)

THE CURSED (*wringing his hands*): Madelon! Madelon! Neither God nor lightning! My crime was therefore not yet great enough.

I who hoped for proofs in the punishment! I'm drowning, Madelon! Ice cold water rises to my mouth! Madelon! You will have the jewels, and in exchange, I will have the doubt. In the presence of terrible doubt all miseries are but delights. Madelon, cover me with your robe, I'm cold. (*He throws himself at the feet of the Prostitute.*)

THE PROSTITUTE (*radiant, leaning on him to better look at the ciborium*): Gold, emeralds, the big diamond...

THE JEW (*dropping the ciborium which falls to the ground, and putting on his cap*): Smoke, Madam, illusion!... He wanted to rob God, and it is God who robs him... *Everything is false.*

An Echo (*very far away*): Wrong!

(*Fading of the decor and the characters.*)

THE HARVEST OF SODOM

For Maurice Maeterlinck

On this dawn, the earth was smoking like a vat filled with an infernal obligation, and the vine, located in the center of the immense plain, was gleaming under an already ferocious rising sun, a purple sun with ember hair which was fermenting in advance the enormous clusters, whose orbs, of a supernatural size, took on the reflections of rolling eyes, all black and sprung from their sockets. Pushed from the bottom of a boiling abyss of bitumen, this vine spread its foliage of gold and blood with an abundance of monstrous richness, and its mad branches ran, twisted like precious metals in fusion around its grapes which piled up on the soft clay, the blond clay, an extraordinarily red carnal earth giving off the scents of fresh sap mixed with pestilential hot mists. Like the beast that is too fertile, that no bond should hinder at the painful hours of multiple births, she rolled on the ground with frightful convulsions, throwing furious streams of garlands, imploring arms stretched out towards the sun, seeming both suffering and delirious with a guilty but heavenly joy, while the overheated marrow overflowed from her, flooding her with a dew of thick tears. She gave birth anywhere to these prodigious fruits of a lustrous, velvety brown, mysterious blossoming of the mortal bitumen, recalling it by their charcoal shade, their shade of satanic sugar distilled through the violence of a volcano. And from certain half-rotten bunches, with skins bursting into scarlet slits, flowed an abominably sweet liquor which intoxicated the bees to the point of killing them. Between the clouds, so red that one would have said they were on fire, and the plain, so yellow that one would have thought it powdered with saffron, nothing sang, nothing stirred; only a dull hum of greedy insects made the vine quiver like a boiling chamber. In the middle of this forest of golden branches, in the primitive press (a colossal trough of rough granite pierced with a round hole, like the altar of human sacrifices), a fabulous lizard, covered with scales of sparkling green and darting a singular hyacinth gaze, lengthened enigmatically, his silver belly heaving from time to time by a panting breath, until, drunk, he too died.

Little by little the clouds grew opalized, turned white, stripped of their appearance of vapors of fire, tore apart, vanished palely; then the sky condensed into a single sun, the azure took on a glow of blued iron burning silently and poured torrents of limpid heat. As far as the eye could see stretched this country of Judea where the spindly fig trees could float on light veils of shadow. Some of these stunted trees, with fingered and hairy leaves, were deformed into the whims of plants dissatisfied with their fate, entwined inextricably their shiny branches covered with transparent excrescences of gum and encircled with bracelets of amber. With stalks leaning from the fire above to the fire below, they had the supple outlines of overwhelmed innocents. Far away, on the horizon, behind the last clump of shrubbery, dominating the vague line of a wall protecting a city, stood a tower of ivory stones, white as bone, a giant tower which fled in spiral towards the deep skies, towards the violet skies, a path leading to infinity and which was further fled by the spire of a flight of great white birds seeking to land on its summit.

From the distant tower came those of Sodom coming towards the vineyard.

They were led by an old man of two hundred years, a funereal colossus towering above them all with his wildly shaky, bony head, hairless and without teeth, from which dangled the ends of a linen drapery. At the corners of his stiff limbs hung this drapery like a shroud. Father, chief and patriarch, over the troop of his posterity, his head had the aspect of an oblong star, shining with moonlight. He was making signs with a stick, not speaking for a long time. At his side crowded his eldest sons, sturdy men with large black beards. One of them, whose name was Horeb, wore, hanging from his tawny leather belt, sparkling goblets which clashed melodiously. Next came a younger group made up of those led by Phaleg, an almost naked, hairless giant, flesh smooth as pink-veined marble, with a beard of brutal red. That one carried on his head a pyramid of wicker baskets in which they had placed wheat cakes. At a respectful distance, the teenagers played with each other, dressed in short dresses, belts adorned with bizarre embroidery, and they threw back their abundant hair, their blond hair like women's fleeces. The most beautiful of them, a child with a purple mouth, violet eyes, his coloring hidden from the mystery of the horizons, was called Sineus, and he had naively festooned his narrow lambskin skirt with flowers. When he entered the vineyard, bees, detaching themselves from the bunches, foraged on his shoulder, bees which, taking him for a honeycomb, so blond he was, tried to draw from his virgin flesh, without hurting him.

After singing a hymn of joy, the pickers began to fill the baskets. The elders, with a slow movement, always the same, picked the heavy grapes. The younger ones rushed in, ravenous, with cries. For a moment, the old man, seated on the edge of the granite trough, got up, stretched out his stick, and everyone came in crowds to empty the full baskets; then the old man sat down again, shaking his brow, and the troop left, carrying away the empty baskets. Some splashed their legs with vermilion juice in spite of themselves, others voluntarily smeared their chests. Sineus furiously trampled the harvest, mixing in handfuls of wild roses. Towards noon, all being tired, they fell asleep side by side, at the knees of the father, and the old patriarch, remaining on the edge of the tub in his motionless posture of a statue, appeared, before these buxom males dripping with wine, the sovereign image of eternal death.

Then, from the next clump of fig trees, a strange creature emerged, stealthily: a woman. She was thin, pale, naked, and so red, so downy, that she seemed clothed in immaculate linen embroidered with gold threads. Her forehead stood out against the azure of the sky, clean and polished like the blade of a dazzling sword; her hair swept the earth, sweeping around the yellow leaves which rattled; her round, peach-like heels barely rested on the ground, and she walked, jumping, with the gait of a cheerful animal. But the two buttons of her breasts were black, a burnt black that was frightening. She approached the sleeping Sineus, first ate all the grapes from his basket, which he had forgotten to empty; and, the grapes having been bestially devoured, she lay down beside him, crawling like a snake. Soon the child woke up, having felt that impure fingers were appropriating his flesh; he gave a lamentable groan, got up, pushed the woman away, and to his tearful cries answered the furious roars of all his brothers. The old man stood up, extended his staff against the intruder as if he could see with his eyes of death. Everyone surrounded the woman. She was one of those prowlers of love whom the wise men of Sodom had driven from their city. In just and formidable anger, men of God had come together to get rid of these mad women, who were haunted from dusk to dawn with a craving for evil passions. Manly, condemning themselves to a chastity of several years so as not to give the best of their strength, during harvest time, to those abysses of pleasure that were the daughters of

Sodom, keeping only the mothers in labor and the old women, they had repudiated even their wives, even their sisters. And so these women had come out of the crossroads, had fled from the streets, bruised by beatings, their breasts torn, without clothes. They had been chased like dogs. Launched across the desert, they had rushed towards Gomorrah through the burning sands. Many had died in the furnace of the plain. Some lived by plundering the vineyards. Yet none of these accursed repented, for their bodies, whipped with insane desires, enjoyed the flames of the sun and possessed a sex as ardent as the secrets beneath the earth.

Now, one of these female dogs was once again asserting her appetites for males by attacking a child who looked like her.

"Who are you?" asked Horeb.

"I am Sarai!"

Sineus veiled his face in his bent elbow.

"What do you want?" said Phaleg.

"I'm thirsty!"

Ah! She was thirsty! They looked at each other, but their father, fierce, raised his staff, and each bent down to grab a stone.

The woman, fair skinned like the sun, stretched out her arms like two rays.

She cried out, in such a shrill accent that they recoiled:

"Woe to you!"

"Yes, I recognize you," says Horeb, "you stripped me, one night, of my most beautiful cups of metal."

"Me," cried Sineus, tears on the edge of his eyelids, "I don't know you, not having wanted to know you!"

The old man dropped his stick.

"Let her be stoned!" they all roared.

The woman didn't have time to run away. Thirty stones flew at her.

Her breasts burst into red showers, and her forehead was crowned with strips of purple. Leaping, writhing, she tangled her hair with the vine branches that held her prisoner; then she made herself small, very small, crawled, humbly serpentine, slipped into the vat where the must was fermenting, and, pulling onto herself heaps of crushed grapes, she remained inert, increasing the blood of the grapes with the exquisite wine of her veins. As she was still dying, they descended into the trough and trampled her under foot, while prodigious black orbs with the reflections of rolling eyes looked on, with the gaze of a supreme curse.

In the evening, having finished their holy task, the pickers shared the wheat cakes and filled their cups. Disdainful of removing the corpse, all drunk already, more intoxicated by the slaughter than by the vintage, they drank, blaspheming the woman and the horrible poisoned liquor of love; and that very night, while the howls of unknown beasts resounded in the distance, while the atmosphere was saturated with an odor of sulfur, while the giant tower took on the pallor of a skeleton under the gloomy light of the moon, those of Sodom committed, for the first time, a sin against nature in the arms of their younger brother Sineus, whose soft shoulder had the flavor of honey.

THE PROWLER

For Camille Lemonnier

An isolated house in the countryside. Night is falling. In a large dark kitchen, three servants, OLD ANGÈLE, BIG MARTHE, *and* LITTLE CÉLESTINE *are peeling beans. Their mistress,* MADAME, *enters and approaches them with uncertain gestures.*

OLD ANGÈLE (*jokingly*): Do you want to help us, Madame? Oh! There's work to be done!

BIG MARTHE (*stirring the heap of beans and spreading them out on the table*): There you go! We've got enough for until midnight, and a good worker wouldn't get in the way.

LITTLE CÉLESTINE (*sniffing the handful of beans she's holding*): If only the pods didn't smell of rat's pee. But they come from the attic, and up there, those filthy beasts don't get in each other's way! (*She laughs.*)

Madame (*sorrowful*): Light the candle, my poor girls. You'll go blind without it!

Little Célestine (*rushing*): Yes, I said as much. The days have shortened. The sun sets nice and early. (*She lights a tall candle which she places on the table.*)

Madame (*sitting down under the eaves of the fireplace, behind the maids*): If you would close the French window in the dining room, Célestine.

Little Célestine (*surprised*): Why is that, Madame? It's not yet nine o'clock.

Madame (*speaking to herself*): We are single women, after all!

Big Marthe (*stopping peeling*): Have you heard something, Madame? You are acting quite funny...

Old Angèle (*raising her head and examining Madame*): Is dinner not sitting well with you?

Madame (*fidgeting in her chair*): Ah! do you find me pale? No! No! I am not ill. It's probably the road, it's so white in the middle of these black lands, it's so long. I have looked at it for too long. I would like if our house was not by the side of the road.

Little Célestine: As for the road, she has a pretty tail ribbon, that's the pure truth. (*She sits down.*)

Old Angèle (*shaking her head*): And if thieves came one evening, we would have time to see them arrive, yes!

BIG MARTHE (*pompous*): The thieves, today, no longer come by the main roads; they take the little side roads.

LITTLE CÉLESTINE (*laughing, but less loudly*): Is that what Madame is worried about, prowlers, that has her frowning?

MADAME (*dryly*): You are a fool! A forty-year-old woman is afraid of nothing. No! I was just cold, all of a sudden, between my two shoulders...

OLD ANGÈLE: You have to put some sage on to boil, and drink a good cup of it with honey.

MADAME (*rising*): It suddenly took hold of me, while I was looking at the road, over there, on the side of the big walnut tree, and it seemed to me...

LITTLE CÉLESTINE (*curiously*): What did it seem to you, Madame?...

MADAME (*slowly*): That it is sometimes necessary to have a man at home.

BIG MARTHE (*vivaciously*): Ah! I've always said that Madame should remarry. We can't live without a man, at the end of the day!

OLD ANGÈLE (*tearfully*): Oh! if our master hadn't died... it would be better.

LITTLE CÉLESTINE (*sourly*): Of course! We would be more at ease here, and Madame would have to push herself a little, if it were only for the rest of us!

Madame (*dreaming*): Or a dog... a dog barking at night...

Big Marthe (*grousing*). But Madame has said that they eat more than they're worth!

Madame (*trembling*): No, no, no dog, he would only have to bark at night... and that would be awful! (*She paces the kitchen.*) Anyway, all four of us, here, what would we do against a prowler?

Little Célestine: It seems that at the Claudins' there was a bad man who entered through the attic, came down at night when everyone was sleeping, and found an open door and ran away...

Madame: Without doing any harm?

Little Célestine: No!

Madame: Without making noise?

Little Célestine: Not at all! He had his shoes in his hands.

Madame (*very nervous*): So! Did anyone see or hear him?

Little Célestine (*with conviction*): No one. (*Moment of silence.*)

Old Angèle (*in a dull tone*): In my time, I also met a bad boy. I was going to draw water from a well, at the very end of the village. And when cranking, I felt it was heavy, heavy... there was a man in the bucket. He had hid there to scare me... and when I got him up, he said to me...

MADAME (*interrupting*): Listen! All of that is nonsense. You are three and there are three doors to close here. Run each to close one. Too bad if it's not nine o'clock... We're not expecting anything this evening... (*She walks feverishly.*) The French window in the dining room has been repaired... The corridor door has a big padlock bar... And then, upstairs, the gallery door is full of bolts... A prowler couldn't demolish all these doors. (*She turns to the servants.*) Come on, go quickly...

BIG MARTHE (*in a bad mood*): Thank you very much, I'm not going alone. I have to hold the clapper while I put on the bars.

(*All three throw their beans on the table.*)

LITTLE CÉLESTINE (*shuddering*): It's true that it's starting to get cold.

MADAME: You're pretty cowardly! So go ahead together, but be quick and don't forget to look towards the big walnut tree. I'll be waiting for you here.

(*They go out after lighting a lantern.*)

BIG MARTHE (*raising her voice to enter the dining room*): Oh! How dark it is in this filthy house!

OLD ANGÈLE (*raising the lantern with a trembling hand*): You must take a good look. But don't go out.

LITTLE CÉLESTINE (*leaning out of the French window*): Well, what? The big walnut tree, it's still in its place.

BIG MARTHE (*quickly closing the shutters*): That's good! But not so loud. The trees are sneaky.

(*They come back in haste to the kitchen and jostle to get in all three abreast.*)

LITTLE CÉLESTINE (*feverishly*): I looked, Madame, I leaned out, I didn't seen anything. He can come, it's over.

MADAME (*annoyed*): Who is this *He*?

OLD ANGÈLE: The prowler that Madame was saying!

MADAME (*exasperated*): And the corridor door? And the door to the gallery?

BIG MARTHE: Go! Go! Let us catch our breath. (*She wipes her forehead with her apron.*)

MADAME: (*addressing Célestine*): Well, didn't you see anything?

LITTLE CÉLESTINE (*panting*): No... that is to say, I saw the big walnut tree...

MADAME (*anxious*): And then?

LITTLE CÉLESTINE: And then... I think I saw something hiding.

MADAME (*triumphant*): There, do you hear! Something hiding!... Me too, I thought I saw that. Surely, the prowler who would like to enter our house would not start by showing himself...

THE THREE SERVANTS (*together*): Surely!

MADAME (*with authority*): Come on, hurry up! The two others! We must not give him time to enter, so that after that we lock him in here.

(The three servants rush from the side opposite the dining room in a huge corridor, and all of a sudden LITTLE CÉLESTINE *utters a shrill cry.)*

OLD ANGÈLE: Well, what? Holy Virgin! Is it our last day?

BIG MARTHE (*raising* CÉLESTINE *who has fallen*): You haven't finished cooking your turkey, have you? (*She cuffs her.*)

LITTLE CÉLESTINE (*distraught*): I stepped on a toad... yes... I'm sure felt it... it was soft!... (*She cries.*)

OLD ANGÈLE (*searching with the lantern*): It's not a toad, it's a bean pod... These are some unnatural stories, all the same!... (*She grumbles.*)

(All three throw themselves at the door. LITTLE CÉLESTINE *gropes for the bar;* BIG MARTHE *pushes the door;* OLD ANGÈLE, *very troubled, raises the lantern facing the wrong way.)*

OLD ANGÈLE: I can't see anymore.

BIG MARTHE: What's that, looming outside?

LITTLE CÉLESTINE: Ah! my God, I feel an arm lifting my petticoats underneath.

Big Marthe (*screaming*): Madame! Madame! We shall slam the door! (*To old Angèle.*) You throw the light, old owl!

(Old Angèle *turns her lantern upside down, and then* Little Célestine *notices that she has put the bar between the two leaves, which prevents them from joining. She pulls it back without daring to explain anything.*)

Big Marthe (*with a vigorous impulse*): That's it! He's run away!... (*she padlocks the door*) For sure, there was someone...

(*All three come back and rush into the kitchen, then fall back on their chairs, turning pale.*)

Madame (*looking weak*): Why are you shouting? It's terrible to hear you screaming like that in this corridor! I will go with you to the gallery door. I don't want to leave you alone now.

Little Célestine (*dreaming*): It might be true that only we were pushing the door...

Big Marthe: If it's true... damn it... I'm tired of it!

Old Angèle (*shivering*): Here's an evening of misfortune! And there's no more oil in our lantern.

Madame (*resolutely seizes the candle*): Follow me! Let's not waste our time. He might look for another door, if he hasn't already entered!

(*The four women head back towards the corridor, which they cross to take a worm-eaten staircase on the left.* OLD ANGÈLE *has drawn out her rosary.* CÉLESTINE *weeps, rubbing her knee. Upstairs,* MADAME *leans over the banister, she listens.*)

LITTLE CÉLESTINE (*in an unsteady voice*): Someone up there?

BIG MARTHE: It's the echo of the vault. It's nothing!

OLD ANGÈLE (*quivering*): Yes, we're going up. I who am a little deaf, I hear it, sure as the word of the gospel! Blessed Virgin! We'll go up stealthily! We should get out of here altogether. You see, Madame, one can only be safe under the sky.

MADAME (*raising the torch*): We don't need to go down again, by the way. Let's go to the gallery, and, since it has its two staircases at both ends, we'll see…

(*They cross another corridor, then find themselves in front of a door wide open on a large wooden gallery. It's cool, the countryside is peaceful, but there's no moon.*)

MADAME: By closing this door, we won't be able to escape him, if he's *inside!* (*She listens and looks again behind her.*) Look, my poor girls, courage! Try to hear something, those who have a keen ear!

BIG MARTHE (*in a low voice*): I hear someone breathing!

OLD ANGÈLE: Me too!

LITTLE CÉLESTINE: Me too!

(*Suddenly, the three servants rush onto the gallery,* BIG MARTHE *and* LITTLE CÉLESTINE *whirl down the staircase while* OLD ANGÈLE, *at the other one, descends as quickly as her knocking legs allow her.* MADAME *remains dismayed for a moment, a cold sweat runs from her temples. Finally, unable to bear it any longer, she plants her candle on the threshold, rushes after* OLD ANGÈLE. *And all these women, their arms in the air, their puffy skirts, flee haphazardly into the dark countryside, while, like a funeral taper, the candle continues to burn on the gaping threshold of the abandoned house.*)

THE TOOTH

For Albert Samain

PASSING by chance the dining room, she saw, on a sideboard, a dozen pistachio croquets, and, mechanically raising her hand to the silver dish that supported the appetizing pyramid, she chose the nicest, the one with the most icing, with an inexplicable gluttony... since this was not greed. Suddenly, while crunching the cake, she felt a hard object, a small object much harder than the pistachios, and at the same second a vibration ran through her whole body, a strange vibration that went in a spiral from her gums to her heels. What? What was this? She pulls it out with the tips of her two fingernails. What! A pebble in the good baker's croquet! She approaches the pale green stained-glass window, behind which extends a dreamy countryside, all green and all pale, then she examines the pebble very closely, with a slight cold breath on her neck. It's a tooth!

Horror makes her unsteady; she falls to her seat, her pupils dilated. A tooth! Hers? No, no, it's impossible! Why, she would have suffered by now, and she never even had a toothache. She is still young, she takes scrupulous care of her mouth, while having, it must be admitted, a profound disgust for the dentist. She feels there, on the side, a little behind her smile, and finds that there is a hole. She leaps up, strikes the stained-glass window with her forehead, stares irritably at this little object which gleams with a slightly yellowish whiteness. Yes, indeed, it is her tooth; crowned with a dark border at the place of the break. Decayed, but for how long? Attacked by what? At first it causes her no pain, but now she finds herself plunged into one of those despairs which, for lasting only a day, are all the more terrible: she now has a blemish! A door has just opened on her thoughts, and she will no longer be able to speak certain words which will spring, without her warning it, from her mouth. She is not old; yet Death has just given her a first flick.

Throwing the remains of the cursed croquet on the black and white checkerboard, the funeral tiling of the dining room, she flees as if she knew she was being pursued forever. In her room, carefully pulling her door closed, she locks herself in and leans over the mirror. Just a tooth! Calm down! It's not so bad. She tries to laugh out loud, and she turns around terrified. Eh? who is laughing like that? Who laughs with a shadow between their lips? It's her! Oh! This black star in the middle of the double white flash! Nothing can make it disappear. And already she's so far away from the time when she could be laughing out loud. A wrinkle would be something *more*; a gray hair would be a *new* thing. The lost tooth is an irremediable catastrophe; and if she asked the dentist to reset her own tooth, it would still be a false tooth! Oh! She really felt, when it fell from between the pieces of the croquet, as if a little cold heart had escaped from her. She has just expired entirely in a tiny detail of her person. Oh! The terrible reality! Let's go! Let's go! Be brave! She is a reasonable woman, she will not cry, she will not say anything, she will only have this inner exclamation of terrible sorrow: "Lord! Lord!" for she is pious and has made herself a second husband in God, in her supreme moments of despondency. When her mother died, she cried, "Lord!" internally also, in this same way. Tomorrow, when she approaches the sacraments, she will have greater fervor, that's all, and won't think about it anymore.

Unfortunately, her tongue still thinks about it! From the tip of her tapering tongue, she performs senseless rummaging in this dark corner of her jaw. She notices a formidable breach in it, and suddenly, poor woman, she has the very absurd vision of a castle in ruins that she once contemplated during her honeymoon. Yes... she sees the tower over there, a tower which bears a crenellated crown on its summit and which, in the storm clouds, sits like the uneven jaw of a colossal old woman...

Her temples buzz. If her husband was there, she would tell him everything. Besides, he is so discreet, so good, that she really hopes... to hide everything from him. She walks, tries to calm down by closing her eyes in front of the mirror. So it's over, she won't laugh anymore. She will no longer open her mouth wide to swallow an oyster. Suddenly she stops... And what of love?... Oh! What diabolical joy seizes her to think that she can no longer indulge in the wild kisses of her honeymoon! And to think that there are women who take lovers to try to remember those caresses! How much preferable virtue seems to her today. She rushes to a drawer, searches for a little round case, takes out the ring, then, with almost maternal care, filled with superstitious fear, she places her tooth on the black velvet. How white she is, this little dead girl! Who killed her? She is still so healthy, despite the brown border. My God! So is it true? You just go away a little every day, and the horrible thing is that there is no other cause for this inexorable departure, bit by bit, than this: healthy people must nevertheless die one day. Oh! Right now! A revolver! Poison! She wants to leave completely. And a kind of inner echo answers her: "You're no longer whole!"

Before she takes communion the next day, she no longer answers her husband familiarly, out of delicacy. He is a serious, affectionate man, full of pretty attentions without being in love in the least. She has a half smile. "Yes, I was meditating... Come on, don't tease me, now!" He sits down opposite her, pats his thigh for a moment. He wants to talk, to tell a story, her eyes shine. He has met the groundskeeper of Monsieur de la Silve, of that imbecile de la Silve... And he speaks quickly, to have time to say everything before the polite dismissal. He is at odds with de la Silve, the owner of the adjoining estate, and he never forgets to denigrate his dogs, his cars, his livery. Back in Paris, they will once again be excellent friends in their circle, but on holiday they cannot stand each other, because one, the neighbor, has finer pheasants.

Standing, in front of him, she wonders if, out of Christian humility, she should reveal everything to him. But why deteriorate in his eyes? Her confessor won't force her. And listening to him, she feels enveloped in an icy atmosphere. They are two, but she is alone. So there is nothing that you can take with you, two married souls, beyond the bodies? And suddenly a sentence rang out like a shot in her distracted ears. Her husband has just said to her, very gently, moreover: "You see, Bichette, I'm saving a tooth for that idiot from La Silve!" She leans back to her full height on her lounge chair. A nervous breakdown twists her. "Bichette! What's the matter with you? Sacrebleu!" She doesn't answer. He runs to the bell, which does not vibrate for some unknown reason, but, while running, he breaks a crystal wine glass and the chambermaid appeared, frightened. Now they unlace her and she is alone; he withdraws, not asking for explanations, knowing that she is still nervous on the eve of her devotions. She remains alone, she will sleep alone. Oh! So alone with this ridiculous secret!

And the next day she woke up bathed in sweat, having had strange nightmares: it seemed to her that she was chewing her own flesh. She prays, she dresses, forbids anyone to put a scarf on her, chooses a thick veil, puts the round case in her pocket. She doesn't want to part with it. What if they search her articles? She leaves the leafy park by a hidden exit, stealthily reaches the church. The old priest, a country priest, a heavy man, thinks he should greet her before beginning his mass. Finally, he is waiting for her, the host between his big raised fingers; she murmurs: "My God, give me the oblivion of these vanities!" And she advances, eyelids half-closed, kneels. Oh! Oblivion and Consolation! Her whole being tends towards the land of mystical union, where kisses do not question the number of teeth. She receives the host, closes her mouth; but while her tongue, with an unctuous and respectful movement, gently turns over the slice of divine bread, folds it in two to swallow it more quickly, she guesses, she *sees* that God is stopping. He's not used to her yet, and lets himself be held back by a corner, catching on the side of the little breach! The poor woman calls to her aid all she has of saliva. She leaves the Holy Altar in a panic, having the sacrilegious desire to spit, despite her fervor. What! Is it the God of charity who inflicts such a humiliation on her? If it were *ordinary* bread, she would understand, but *His body*! Then she snatches it away with a brutal flick of her tongue, and swallowing suddenly occurs. God disappears, rushes down as if he had been afraid, after having seen. Her face in her clenched hands, she cries. This ends up relieving her. Going back down the shady path in the park, she cries again, although less desperate. A kind of astonishing dryness rises from her heart to her eyes. It is necessary that death announces itself from time to time, otherwise happy people would not think of it; and she contemplates a lily that stands there, under a fir tree with trailing branches, a lily whose sickly whiteness reminds her of that of her dead tooth. With a deep sigh, she takes the little round case out of her pocket, kisses it, digs in the ground, pushes in the tiny coffin that contains this first piece of her. Ungloved, she presses with all the strength of her nervous hands, brings back the moss around the lily, erases the traces of the burial; then, with trembling lips, she walks away, a little earth under her nails...

PLEASURE

For Camille Mauclair

A spring morning. A clearing in a wood. In the middle of a thick carpet of moss, a large round fountain, like an enormous moon of water. Clouds pass by from time to time, shimmering with singular reflections on the peaceful plain sheet, and then the day seems to emerge from the earth while the shade of the trees obscures the sky. Around the fountain mottled insects rustle, flies of a sparkling green, very small blue butterflies striped with black. Exquisite scents of wild violets. The two lovers, SHE *fourteen,* HE *fifteen, are sitting near the water; they stare at the moss, not daring to look too much at themselves. They're worried.*

SHE: These are things we'll never understand, since we can't ask our parents.
HE: Is it very useful to understand?

SHE: You're stupid! You, a man, you should know.

HE: I'm still just a... boy.

SHE: Well, I can't stand the way you look! (*She makes a gesture of impatience.*)

HE (*suddenly angry*): And I hate the way you speak!

(*Silence.*)

SHE (*dreaming*): No! It's not natural, everything that happens to us. Recently, while reading in my Mass book: "*And Jesus, leaning his head, gave up his soul,*" my whole body shivered. Why did I tremble like this? I don't know, but it almost gave me pleasure to be in pain and to feel sorry for God. (*She turns to her lover.*) Do you want me to tell you everything that's been bothering me since we've known each other? You, will you tell me what amuses you? This will be our game today.

HE (*sulky*): I don't mind.

SHE: I've started, your turn.

HE (*sighing*): Me, I often stand still in front of a pane of my window thinking of you, who hardly deserve it, then I want to run my fingernail along the glass to make it screech, and just thinking about that my mouth fills with saliva. I have to make my fingernails screech, it's stronger than me, I have to! The panes attract my fingernails. (*He spits.*)

SHE: You're telling me what pains you. I asked you what made you happy.

HE: No, it's a pleasure! I assure you. You just told me that crying over the Good Lord amuses you!

SHE: Oh! I have even prettier sorrows, like so! When I wash, I press my sponge above my neck and gently let drops flow. They roll slowly, with little hateful chills, then they end up burning me, and I fall back into an armchair, seized with a fit of laughter! Oh! it's a terrible pain, that one! I could never stop giving it to myself...

HE: It's not funny, indeed! I have another even more beautiful pleasure. I put my index finger under a razor, and I say to myself: "One! Of them! Three!... Watch out!" Then I immediately remove the razor when I feel it is going to cut. I think I see my blood dripping on the floor, and my finger fall wriggling like a piece of red snake. Ah! If they saw me, they would know that I have courage. Each time, moreover, I split my skin a little, a very little bit.

SHE: The other morning, I picked a lily in the garden, a lily full of dew. First I shook off the dew... because of the birds; and I filled it with fresh milk. It was foaming! It foamed! It looked like white champagne, and it smelled of warm flowers. Unfortunately, my lily burst at the bottom, and the milk spilled on my dress. I almost sobbed immediately thinking that some little children don't always have good milk to drink.

HE (*affectionately*): Yes, that's good of you, it's a charitable thought. (*With curiosity.*) Why did you shake off the dew? Dew isn't dirty.

SHE (*very dignified*): Do you want me to drink after all the warblers in the country?

HE: (*naively*): But the milk? You drank it after the calf, since cows have calves before they have milk?

SHE (*disdainfully*): No! how stupid you are! As if we needed to talk about veal right now.

HE (*confused*): I can't find any other pleasure. Too bad for the game.

SHE (*peremptorily*): Look for them.

HE (*making an effort*): I like pure wine. It hurts my head, but I drink it all the same.

SHE: What a stupid pleasure! Besides, no one is forbidding you. For me, when I eat too much, I think I no longer look like angels, and if I were free I would only dine with babes!

HE (*searching*): Wait a minute. You are going so fast! (*He yawns.*) Ah! I have one! I found a mouse in my closet the other day, I grabbed it by the tail to kill it and it turned around to bite me, so I let it go. I was very happy to let it go .

SHE (*laughing*): Naughty fool! To get bitten by a mouse! You have to come and find my green-eyed cat. She loves them so much! With a single stroke of her paw she removes the skin from their heads, and we see them running around in every corner with a little ruby cap!

HE (*very quickly*): And then! And then! Oh! I still have all sorts of beautiful pleasures... When I go to bed, I put your portrait under my bolster, and I fall asleep calling you *my little wife*. And then!... (*He stops embarrassed.*) Decidedly, no, these are not pretty pleasures, and I'd rather not tell you about them... There are things just for me.

SHE: Sometimes, I play on my piano my easiest waltz very quickly, as if I were turning and the keyboard was in a circle around me; and a passage where there is a high note, I repeat it for hours, I manage to hit only one chord, only this single high note, always, always, until my wrist begins to burn. It becomes like a noise of crystal that is perpetually broken, it's fine, fine, and it tells me extraordinary things. It enters my ear like a curled feather, a diamond aigrette, a velvet brush. The other night, if Mama hadn't come to the living room, I was going to drop dead and I would have broken into two pieces... Ah! There is the penalty of satin. I run my hands over my pompadour satin foot cover, and... you know, we have little *desires*, little excoriations on the fingertips, so all my flesh bristles so much it hurts me to run them over this so soft fabric. It's like the windows, for you! I can't help it! There's the pain of unripe gooseberries that I eat on the sly, it stings my tongue and it's very bad... The pain of wanting to have a tulle shirt of veil, embroidered with large polka dots, two of which would stop on each of my breasts. The pain of breathing hyacinths! Oh! That one, my darling, you cannot believe how much pleasure it gives me! I'm going to stretch out on the ground right up against a big pink hyacinth that has grown at the bottom of the garden, near a bower. They are in the shadows like here. I throw my dress over my head and wrap my arms around the flower so that the perfume rises entirely in my nose, and I breathe... I breathe... It seems to me that I am eating honey while bees in flight brush my eyelids with their sugar wings! (*She swoons.*) You can't understand anything about it! But it's so delicious that I've forgotten you!

HE (*sucking on a twig he's just pulled out, at random*): Thank you very much! That's a pretty ridiculous invention!

SHE: Do you know what the hyacinth smells like?

HE (*ironic*): It smells of hyacinth, probably.

SHE: No, it smells of my heart!

HE (*annoyed*): So you've already smelled your heart!

SHE: Yes! I'm sure it's a bag filled with bell flowers.

HE (*laughing*): That's not possible! Show it, and I'll see?

SHE (*sighing*): Oh no, you'll never see it! (*Silence.*)

HE (*throws his twig in the water with an angry movement*): You're very bad for me today. We only have these few hours of walking to spend together, and you take advantage of it to overwhelm me!

(*The sparkling flies rise tumultuously from the calm sheet of water and buzz around the two teenagers.*)

SHE (*strongly interested*): Look at the beautiful flies. They look like living, burning emeralds.

HE (*desiring to flatter her*): Or your cat eyes!

SHE: They've just bathed, because they shine like drops of green water! Catch one, say?

HE: And if it stings me!

SHE: It's possible! Don't startle them.

(*They come closer to each other as if to defend themselves against a possible attack*).

He: I don't think they're bad. (*A fly lands on the lover's cheek*). Here! This one takes you for a plant. (*Graciously.*) She felt your heart no doubt. Frrrrrrr... here she goes! And she didn't dare hurt you! (*They look at each other, moved, and kiss furtively.*) Let's make peace! Me, I have no more pleasures to tell you.

She: And me, no more pain to tell you (*At this moment, the clarity of the fountain goes out, the sky darkens.*) Let's play something else!

He (*taking her hands*): Let me unbutton your bodice to smell your heart, I'm tempted!

She (*modestly*): It wouldn't be appropriate.
(*She steps back a little and plays with the water. We hear a sound like pearls being moved.*)

He (*on his knees*): I beg you!... (*He throws some water in her face.*) I want to!
(*She bursts out laughing and leans back, her hair unwinding on the water.*)

She: No! No! Not that, but I'll allow you to caress my pigtails.

He (*rushing to her already wet hair*): Do they smell of hyacinth too? Give them to me! Give me your hands, your little shell hands! Give me your face, give me your height... Hey! Give me everything, since I will never have your heart. (*He dries her hair with his kisses.*)

She: You're unbearable!

He (*looking at her with passion*): I'm thirsty! Give me some of this water in your two hands united, like holy water. It's strange, my lips are burning. (*She draws water and holds out her two full hands to him; he drinks, distraught*). It looks like honey, it looks like milk, it looks like blood, it looks like wine, it looks like brandy. It smells and it clouds. Yes, your hands smell of hyacinth! Oh! How happy I am! (*He gazes at her.*) Listen! I have a way of taking you in spite of yourself entirely. You are going to bend over the fountain and gaze at yourself, then you will give me some water to drink again, which you will take from the place where you will have seen yourself. So I will drink your portrait and you will be in me for eternity! (*Anxiously.*) Does that seem appropriate enough to you?

SHE (*smiling*): Yes, on the condition that I only mirror the top of my face. (*She bends over the water.*) I can't see myself well! Oh! how deep this water is! I bet this fountain crosses the whole earth, it is so black! Ah! I see myself... I see myself... Here! I'm soaking my pigtails in it again, you'll taste my hair, and since I'm very blonde it'll be absolutely honey!

HE (*shyly*): You'll drink me in your turn, you say?

SHE (*with disdain*): I will not drink from the hands of a boy.

HE (*bowing devoutly to her hands, which she has again filled with water*): Oh! I thank you all the same. You are so sweet to me when you want! (*He sniffs the water and sits up proudly.*) Now, I'll take you everywhere.
(*The fountain lights up little by little, the clouds pass, the flies begin to buzz again in the sun.*)

SHE: Was it good?

HE (*intoxicated*): Like the wine of the mass!
(*He rolls at her feet with the joy of a young dog.*)

SHE (*moralizing*) : When our parents marry us, we will build our country house here. It's not too far from town, and the baker can bring us soft bread every day. Me, you see, I wouldn't live without soft bread.

HE (*looking at her from the ground with delight*): Is it true that you think I'm stupid?

SHE (*looking into the water distractedly*): Yes! Yes! We will have a fine barnyard, and we will eat roast chicken every day, except Sundays. Only, you'll kill the chickens, because I'm afraid of blood.

HE: Is it true that you love me?

SHE (*more and more distracted and leaning in different directions*): We'll go up on horseback every morning, I'll have a riding habit of gray cloth... Here! What do I see there, in the middle of this pond? We'll have a maid who will know how to change the shape of my dresses every week, I'll follow the fashions. Finally! What do I see in there? It's dark, dark! It rises to the surface blowing bubbles... (*She gets up.*)

HE (*still stretched out on his back*): Me, I adore you!

SHE: Come on! Get up! We have to go back. My God, this water is crystal clear! She's so blue right now that you'd think she was leaning over a sky fallen into the moss...
(*She comes closer again and lets out a terrible cry that awakens distant echoes.*)

HE (*jumping up*): What's the matter with you, my beloved?

SHE (*turning round in a panic*): Don't come forward, I forbid you!
(*She staggers a few steps, then goes to fall into her arms.*)

HE (*desperate*): She feels bad! My God! She will die! Help!

SHE (*in a broken voice*): It's nothing, darling! Let's move on! (*Her voice drops more and more.*) Take me away without looking at the water, without looking at the water... (*She faints.*)

(THE LOVER *obediently, takes her like a dead woman whose arms hang down inert, while a reflection of the sun illuminates the other dead woman, whose mouth is open wide and her very white teeth are visible through the pure water.*)

THE GHOST TRAP

For Karl Rosenval

WE arrived in front of this house on a very stormy day. The horse that was taking us there stopped every moment, and put its head between its legs to shake off the flies, as if to say to us: "No! Nope! Think. Let's go no further..." Our maid, her hands crossed over a big full basket, rolled her eyes worriedly. My mother questioned the driver of the cart in a trembling voice, and this peasant replied with harsh half-words. My father, holding the bundle of walking sticks and umbrellas, said nothing, as usual, but he seemed very preoccupied. I saw a cord winding along the wall, and thus taking possession of what I already called the *holiday house*. I knew there was no one, since the old gardener, its owner, lived in town; only, at twelve years old, the urge to pull a string is still irresistible, isn't it? And I rang the bell furiously. Then came from behind this wall, adorned with thick foliage, the shrill sound of a church bell, like the shrill laughter of someone crouching in a tree to terrify us. It was both so petty and so disagreeable that I stood dumbfounded, fingers clenched on the stick for my hoop, the stick which I used to put, like a dagger, in my belt.

"Who started laughing?" asked my mother.

"Who pulled the chains?" cried the maid.

The peasant brutally unloaded our four trunks, pell-mell, in the path, then he turned away without wanting to listen to us.

"That's a fine way of introducing us here!" muttered my father, examining rusty keys.

He tried to open the gate, but it did not yield immediately. We had to push hard. Papa got help first from me, and I got help from our maid. Mama was turning pale under her veil, I no longer dared to laugh. I felt, now, that there was something in the air. Suddenly, the gate relaxed like a spring, and we were all three thrown to the ground as we entered. My mother had a nervous fright, declaring that it was better not to go any further. The maid looked around her with a bewildered face; she was rubbing her knees and repeating:

"It smells of death here, Madame, I swear it smells of death!"

"You're crazy!" said my father, annoyed, dragging the trunks.

"No, Marie is right," resumed my mother, "this garden looks like a cemetery."

"Fine, but it was you who wanted to come!" said my father, a little red. "Let's not be ridiculous. What's done is done."

❖

Outside, the place had the very ordinary aspect of a poorly maintained house. It had six large windows with rickety shutters and a doorway with a zinc awning sagging on one side, and had only one ground floor. Above, the roof jutted out like the brim of a dark hat. The garden was garlanded with white bindweed that festooned all the shrubs and jumped from one path to another. As long as the sun was shining, it did not lack charm. Me, I only discovered a messy space very convenient to play. I couldn't damage the baskets or the rare plants, since there was only grass and wild flowers. If it looked like a cemetery, it was still a gay cemetery. But the sun veiled itself in a copper-colored cloud, the greenery took on an ugly hue, and after two or three runs through the bindweed I was in a bad mood.

We put our trunks away inside the hall. Marie opened all the windows, dusted the furniture in the bedrooms, and Mama calmed down. While we were proceeding to our final installation, I had the idea of slipping behind the house by going around the garden, for there was no door leading to the other half of the *cemetery*. To my amazement, I found myself in almost complete darkness. The threatening storm had eaten up the sun, and there remained only a small livid ray illuminating the round pane of an attic skylight. This reflection of a large sick eye in all this gray, all these cracked walls, produced a very singular effect on me. The garden, and the house, on this side, took on a strange aspect, with the colors of a green toad. Bindweed no longer even bloomed on the shrubs. The grass was disturbingly large and wild. Three boxwoods, formerly carved into the silhouettes of Capuchins, stood at intervals, and the last one, at the back, near the high enclosing wall, looked like a sinister man planted with his back turned. And that glassy eye, darting over that corner of virgin forest, wept for God knows what desolation. I started running, screaming fiercely, stamping my feet, trying to react against the secret terror that invaded me, and all the noises died out in plaintive echoes that the trees sent back to each other like words of order. My mother pushed aside a shutter when she heard me scream and gave me imperious signs. I came back, leaping, very happy to know that I was being watched, giving myself victorious airs, brandishing the stick for my hoop:

"You must not shout here!" said my mother, her face very frightened.

"Why, mother? You promised to let me have fun at all the games in the vacation house!"

She added, without answering me directly and as if talking to herself:

"You know we haven't rented this house just for you, my child, it is a sacrifice that you will have to take into account for us, later. You are too young to understand me well; but if I hear you scream, it will get on my nerves!"

A roll of thunder rumbled, and she quickly helped me to climb through the window, murmuring:

"Huh? You see! You shouldn't shout here!"

No shouting, no running, no ringing, no opening the gate... and even the stupid horse which didn't want to move on the road. No! It was beginning to be less fun, the *vacation house*!

❖

All night long the storm shook the roof, and it was a real miracle that the zinc canopy did not completely collapse.

After eight days, we were still not used to this filthy house. Marie, the maid, who was old and impressionable, was complaining because she found rats in the bread basket. She begged me to accompany her to the cellar and the attic, thrusting a candle between my fingers, a candle whose wax which ran down the length of my blouse. One day when I refused to go to the attic with her, Mama followed her there, and, the wind slamming the door behind their backs, they remained locked up in the middle of the darkness for an hour, calling for help. It was becoming obvious that they were afraid of something they knew and I didn't.

The furniture in this dwelling was turning to dust, dating at least from the Merovingian period. When you rubbed it, it made lugubrious sounds, broke apart on its own or shattered.

Then, there were really inexplicable little events, which even now I can't explain to myself, like small objects in this bizarre dwelling disappearing, suddenly swept away as if by magic. Did my mother leave the living room for a minute to give an order to the kitchen? When she came back she couldn't find her dice. No matter how much I squatted in all corners and searched during the afternoon with a light: it was a done deal, the dice were lost. So with embroidery scissors, so with balls of wool. Papa, hoping to relax from his hard work of writing, wanted to garden, and as soon as he handled spades, rakes, shears, he misplaced them. Sometimes it was a pickaxe that ended up, an hour after patient research, in a place where no one had ever put it, sometimes it was a shovel that melted into the shrubs and evaporated completely. My father accused me of playing bad pranks. My mother defended me and repeated:

"Oh! Here, nothing surprises me!" in a low voice, irritated by this thing that I didn't know.

No, these adventures couldn't be explained at all.

One morning, at breakfast, regarding the salt shaker that had just been spilled, mother had a hysterical fit. Marie uttered exclamations of despair.

"Come on," said Papa impatiently, "it's very simple: let's get the hell out of here. Besides, I didn't want to rent, but did so because of your sacred character. You are unreasonable!"

Marie picked up the salt silently, believing that it was spoiling. Me, I started to draw on the butter, with the tip of a knife.

"A whole house almost for nothing!" Mama murmured.

"For nothing, it's highly expensive," Papa said dryly.

The window was wide open, the three capuchin-trimmed box trees stood guard. Mama stretched out her arm.

"They're like ghosts. Do you think they're reassuring?"

Papa tried to reconcile.

"Hey! I will prune them today. Maurice will help me! We will give them the shape of three puppets. Shed of ghosts, it will be a real recreation for the eye. No, Maurice?"

I exclaimed warmly:

"I think so, little father!"

Mama shrugged her shoulders.

"Come on! Will those trees allow themselves to be pruned... You, a pen-pusher, would you like to prune trees, and with a child, yet?"

There was a long embarrassed pause.

Me, I continued to see my penknives, my marbles, my strings, above all my strings, disappear. As soon as I made a whip, the stick I held between my legs to tie it securely ended up vanishing through the coarse grass, and the string, if I turned my head, ran away somewhere. It irritated me. I felt that it was not just *a thief who stole*... And, unless we were all very dazed... *something* was harassing us in this vacation home, certainly. Once, Marie lost some laundry that she had put out to dry on a line, and when I asked her why, she replied, with a serious face:

"You are too young. Madame forbade anyone to tell you about the story."

So there was a story. Oh! Oh! I spent the days racking my brains and losing my strings. My brain worked itself over, little by little. I didn't really believe in nursery tales, because I was going to college, where you learn not to be afraid of dark corners; but I saw mom tremble as soon as dusk invaded the room, and dad was worried, while Marie moaned. All this had to be cleared up as soon as possible, and, if there was an enemy, the family quickly gave in. I resolved to go to our maid to get a full confession. Marie was naive, I was as cunning as a Redskin; we would see which of us would be *too young!* One evening, I arrived in the kitchen walking on tiptoe, looking very mysterious.

"Marie," I said, "look out the window near the last boxwood!"

The maid dropped a coffeepot which she was filling with water and turned her eyes towards the dark window.

"Monsieur Maurice, what is it? Again, Lord God!"

"I saw something at the bottom of the garden, Mary."

"Ah! you saw..." Her teeth chattered. "It was all white, wasn't it?"

"Yes, Marie. All white!"

"And long? And it was dragging? And it extended?" She came closer, very moved, pressed her nose against the window, holding me by the shoulder, so that her shiver communicated to my whole body. "And it writhed in the air like a piece of linen flying away?"

111

"Exactly, Marie, it was like your linen when it flew away. Oh! What I was afraid of!"

"You were sure it had a tall woman's skirts?"

"Yes, Marie, I thought you wore skirts."

"Well! Monsieur Maurice, you've seen the *ghost*, for you're painting his whole portrait for me right now!"

"The ghost, Marie?"

I was a little disappointed. I would have preferred a story about thieves. I had, moreover, *painted his portrait* in spite of myself!

"The ghost, Monsieur Maurice," continued the maid solemnly, "is the lady who died here ten years ago. She lived in the company of a gentleman, without the sacrament, and when the gentleman left her, she hanged herself. The whole country knows the story, so that no one has ever dared to rent the house again, before your mother."

I was dumbfounded. The hanged woman returning from the other world to steal my strings and devour pickaxe handles! Certainly, it was beyond my imagination! I knew what I wanted to know, but I had hardly advanced! In my bed, I had nightmares, and I curled up against the wall, trying to go back to sleep by covering my ears. Grown-ups like my mother and my maid being afraid of the *ghost*! What was to be concluded?

At dawn, my ideas took another course, I no longer wanted to admit that a former hanged woman, very moldy, would come out of her grave to tease a cook by stealing her dishcloths. No! The *ghost* must have been an animal of a particular species, haunting badly enclosed places, especially disorderly houses, and I came to believe that people were talking to me about *a dead woman* so as not to frighten me too much about a real danger! She had confessed everything so easily, that crazy old Marie. Soon the heroic thought of capturing *the beast* filled my brain, dazzling me. I was strong, I was skillful, I had information on the manners of the Indians, and, once on the warpath, I would not back down. What a feat and what an honor! My mother would cry with joy as on the day of the prizes, my father would call me: *proud rabbit*! and Marie could risk picking parsley at dusk. Decidedly, I would fight against the common enemy.

The plan was already mapped out. I would dig a pit which I would cover with various branches, according to the system of American trappers, and when the animal prowled around, during its daily or nightly *returning*, it would not fail to drop right into the hole. Then we would make it throw up the silver dice, the rakes, the penknives and other indigestible food on which it had the deplorable habit of fattening herself. So I dug a rather deep pit, on the side of the last boxwood; I covered it with clods of grass and green twigs. The soil removed was scattered to the four corners of the garden. At nightfall, I finished my dark work, pretending to watch for birds to deceive my parents, for I dreaded their jokes or their defenses. As long as the sun had me, I had sung at the top of my voice, very happy with my chivalrous idea, forming the most rash projects, full of contempt for the *revenant*, who, after all, was only a beast, *which had to be revealed*.

But, in the evening, the sacred garden darkened frightfully, the Capuchin boxwoods took on toad tints, and the sick eye, the skylight of the attic, looked at me, from the top of this sad house, with a horrible expression of despair. I dropped my tools, pickaxe, shovel and rake, I fled abruptly without being able to stop, as if pursued by the last boxwood, which now seemed to be raising its green hood. In front of the house, I sighed for a moment, very ashamed of my terror.

See here! Was I going to lose my beautiful courage? "Are you a chicken?" asked my conscience. If I left the gardening tools there, it would give away that I was playing a prank. Such a well-designed and well-executed trap! I turned to orient myself. The pit was over there, somewhere, between the second and the third Capuchin... Strange thing! In this twilight, I also lost all sense of distance. Was the pit more to the left or more to the right? Eh? What did that mean? Me, a cunning boy, I didn't recognize myself in it anymore! The paths sank, all black, the shrubs twisted with bindweed, undulating like plumes of smoke, the tall trees mingled with the clouds, and the moon, rising, took on the aspect of a yellow eye in the leaves, all at once, in imitation of the attic skylight.

Suddenly, the thought that *over there*, between the second and the last boxwood, there was a *dug pit*, made my hair stand on end. I had dug a pit, me, a tomb, as if to bury a dead person there. A tomb which awaited the hanged woman, *the ghost*! Has a beast ever had the shape and height of a woman trailing skirts! And since Marie had seen her! My blood froze in my veins, my legs wobbled. "Will you go! Won't you go! Chicken!" my conscience was still screaming at me. Finally, seized with I don't know what furious vertigo, I shouted: "Let's go!" And I rushed in a straight line. I even think I was galloping, eyes closed, without looking any further at which way I went, convinced that if I opened my eyes I would surely see the hanged woman at the bend of the clump. Ah! It was no longer a question of a thieving animal, I felt that I was in the power of a mysterious character, *of an unknown person,* who was attracting me, attracting me, smelling me, devouring me from the bottom of this garden-graveyard! And my heart was pounding. Mechanically, I murmured: "I'll bend down, I'll grab the pickaxe, the shovel, one in each hand, I'll be well armed if something happens... Yes! The pickaxe is next to a blackcurrant stalk, and the shovel has remained on a clod of grass. Provided, my God, that these tools have not already gone to *her*! Come on, let's try not to be mistaken... One... two... three... I'm going to open my eyes, too bad, I must be in the right place!" I opened my eyes, and with a cry of distress which must have resounded cruelly in my mother's chest, I also threw up my arms as my legs gave way and I collapsed at the bottom of the pit. The violence of my fall was such that I fainted...

And they found me in there, lying like a dead man, caught in my own trap!

I had a fever for a month. My mother, as soon as I could get out of bed, ordered us to pack our things quickly. She was tired of the *holiday home*, where the graves dug themselves to swallow up the little children, and she never wanted to believe the story of my trap, because I could never prove to her that I had wanted to catch a ghost as one catches a common weasel! Besides, thinking about it a little... isn't it the *revenant* who would have liked to catch me?

A BOTHER

For Louis Dumur

A MAN is about to be born. The guardian Angel, dispatched to his soul, allows him to hesitate before hatching. He hesitates... His mother's childbirth becomes laborious, and during this time the soul of man can study the conditions of his future life.

THE ANGEL: If you are born, you will die. Life is a deadly disease. If you live a lot, you will suffer a lot. If you die young, you will regret existence. Choose!

THE MAN: Damn! What to do? Give me a strong body, meanwhile.

THE ANGEL: If your body is vigorous, its own strength will cause it to wear out. If it wears out, you will contract terrible infirmities. If it does not wear out, it will have confidence in its solidity, and its confidence will cause it to throw itself headlong into the first peril that comes along. If you becomes a soldier, you will be killed in a war. If you becomes an assassin, you will be killed on the scaffold. If you make a maneuver, you will have quarrels with your companions. If you have quarrels, you will want to vent them... and if you vents them, you will take a mortal blow.

THE MAN: Then I ask for a very delicate body.

THE ANGEL: If you are delicate, from childhood all sorts of misfortunes will come to you. You will fall and you will make lumps. If you have lumps, they will leave marks. If you have a bad nurse, you will become comsumptive. Later, if you don't get exercise, your classmates will cheat you over everything. If you don't retaliate, you'll be considered a coward... and if you retaliate you'll be tricked.

THE MAN: Enough! Give me income, that's the main point.

THE ANGEL: No! It is only the interest. If you have annuities, you will want to spend them. If you spend badly, you will feel remorse. If you're miserly, it won't be worth having. If you manage your fortune yourself, you will risk it on a stock market blow. If you manage it, your bankers will slow down. If you entrust it to your parents, they will want you to marry an impossible heiress and you will fall out with them.

THE MAN: Make me poor.

THE ANGEL: If you are poor, you will envy the rich. If you envy them, you will work to match them. If you work, you will want to rest on Sunday. If you rest on Sunday, you'll get tipsy and lazy. If you become lazy, you will become a *communist*, and if you are *communist*...

THE MAN: I will be *socialist*, I will practice honest politics.

THE ANGEL: If you do of honest politics, you will be deceived... then you will pass for a fool.

THE MAN: I prefer to pass for a fool.

THE ANGEL: If you are a fool, your wife will deceive you, and you will have...

THE MAN: I shall have no wife!

THE ANGEL: If you have no wife, you will take mistresses. If you have mistresses, they will ruin your health or your purse. If you don't let them ruin you, they will give you a reputation for being stingy, you will be badly received by society; and your servants will come out of your house saying they are starving there.

THE MAN: I will have no servants.

THE ANGEL: If you have no servants, you must dip your soup and that of your children yourself: you will be ridiculous.

THE MAN: I shall have no children.

THE ANGEL: If you don't you have any children, your old age will be very unhappy, and you will die isolated.

THE MAN: Sacrebleu! I shall have them...

THE ANGEL: If you have them, your old age will be unhappy because of their follies, and you will have the pain of disinheriting them.

THE MAN: It is too strong! Can't one marry a barren woman?

THE ANGEL: If you marry a barren woman, she will complain about you in court, giving particulars...

THE MAN: I shall never be in love.

THE ANGEL: If you are not in love, you will lose half the earthly enjoyments, and, I warn you, there are not many.

THE MAN: Good! I shall therefore be in love... as much as possible.

THE ANGEL: If you are too much, you will begin early. If you start early, you will address yourself the wrong way. If you miss your first heart, yours will wear an eternal shroud (old style). If you love an ingenue, she'll have a cousin in college. If she has a cousin in college, he'll get out... If he gets out, he'll take over, and if he takes over...

THE MAN: I'd like a mature ingenue or a young widow.

THE ANGEL: If she be ingenuous, she will be stupid; if she is ripe, she will be ugly. If you love a young widow, she'll have experience. If she has too much, you won't have enough... she'll find you insufficient, and if...

THE MAN: In any case, I will look for a pretty woman.

THE ANGEL: If she's pretty... you won't be the first to prove it to her.

THE MAN: A devout pretty girl, for instance.

THE ANGEL: If she is devout, she will go to church. If she goes to church, you'll be jealous and you'll never have dinner at the same time. If you're jealous and you don't eat regularly, you'll make a scene for her, so she'll go back to her family. If she returns to her family, she will take her dowry...

THE MAN: I will claim the dowry...

THE ANGEL: Your mother-in-law, on the contrary, will force you to provide her with a pension, and, moreover, she will call you: *executioner of her daughter!*

THE MAN: Oh! Let's leave that subject. I will therefore love as little as possible... I will marry a large, quiet, country girl, and to escape temptations I will live near a village.

THE ANGEL: If you live in the country, you will do agriculture, you will plant vineyards; they will freeze or have phylloxera.

If you have farmers, they won't pay their rents, because their sheep will have *pietain*. If they have oxen, they will sell badly. You will have sharecroppers the second year, when you will see that the tenant farming does not succeed: the sharecroppers are all thieves or lazy. If you find good people, they will get sick. If you have neither farmers nor sharecroppers, your properties will remain *fallow*. If they remain *fallow*, you will be accused of ineptitude, you will not be named municipal councilor. If you're a good landlord and you're named a municipal councilor, you'll want to be mayor. If you're not mayor, you'll cabal. If you are, you'll cabal. If you announce yourself as a Bonapartist, the workers will ask you for a salary increase. If you are a republican, the priest will preach against your schemes and the aristos will close their doors to you. If you are sometimes one, sometimes the other, you will naturally be seated on the floor the day when everyone takes a chair!

The Man: One may have a modest dwelling, near a town, and not set foot in that town. I don't care much for large property.

The Angel: If you are near a town, importunate friends will come to see you, you must invite them to dinner... If they dine often, it will cost you dear!...

THE MAN: Ah! my God! I won't see anyone, I'll have a walled garden, a deaf gardener, a mute cook, and... I'll read the newspapers to get bored.

THE ANGEL: If you don't see anybody, they will think you have reasons to hide. If your garden has walls, they'll climb them at night to discover your crimes... and take your pears. If your gardener is deaf, he will not hear; if your cook is mute, she won't say so. If you read the newspapers in such solitude, you will go mad after six weeks. You will learn that closed houses and closed gardens are suspect, that *Freemason*... or women, will generally gathered there. Fate will want a strangled newborn to be deposited in the sunken path along your walls: if they find him, they will raid your house. The deaf and the mute will accuse you, one by his incoherence, the other by desperate signs. If you defend yourself seriously, you are very guilty. If you don't defend yourself, you are despicable. Those who have stolen your pears will give certain proofs. There will arrive, just in time, a little prankster milkmaid whose chin you will have forgotten to stop from wagging, one morning when she was ready to grant you the last favors. To take revenge, she will declare one of her 26 pregnancies, and you will be stuffed inside. If you have allowed yourself to follow the *Gazette des Tribunaux* more attentively than the *Revue des Deux-Mondes*, it will be thought that you were already looking for your system of defense. All you have to do is get a good lawyer, who will have you sent to the galleys by pleading the extenuating circumstances; and if you go to prison, you'll end up believing yourself to be a criminal... you'll die there confessing fabulous stories.

THE MAN: You have nothing attractive, then, it seems to me?

THE ANGEL: If you have genius, you will be misunderstood. But if you don't, you will be unknown. If you are a pianist, you will be the desolation of your neighbors, and they will attach bacon to your bell cord. A painter, you will take twenty-five years to choose a school for yourself, and, in your old age, deciding on yours, you will make your comrades giggle, who will call you: *old monk*! An actor, you will be hissed; if you are not hissed, you will have all the great ladies on your arms, and all their husbands or their lovers on your back. A writer, you will seek publishers; if you don't find any, you'll starve; if you find any, they will ask you to *compromise* the situation; if you make it harder, you'll be accused of pornography; if you stick to your ideals and refuse this slight sacrifice to your editor, he will treat you as *monsieur annoying*. You will never be published if you write in verse; if you write in prose, the influential *journalists* will take care to *criticize* your books to prevent them from pleasing the public, which, certainly, they would have pleased without these benevolent criticisms. I add that if you are immoral, you will go prison, and that if you are moral, you will stun the whole world!

THE MAN (*explosively*): Decidedly, I'm going back into nothingness, but... one more word: what if I were a scientist or a philosopher?

THE ANGEL: (*gravely*) If you want to be a scholar and a philosopher, for almost a century you will have to drink in disappointments, arm yourself with patience, go from disagreement to disagreement, deny love, deny friendship, deny wealth, deny pleasures, to deny even God, all this to end up concluding that: if you had not been born, you would not have been unhappy!

THE MAN: Servant!

(*The labors of the young woman are more and more industrious. Soon, the doctor rolls a small corpse in a cloth, then the poor exhausted mother falls asleep, while her doctor murmurs: "If they had called me yesterday!"*)

THE PANTHER

For Laurent Tailhade

FROM the underground passages of the circus the cage slowly ascended, dragging with it a thick piece of night, and when the gates opened to the resplendent light of the heavens, the beast which, suddenly finding under her feet the golden mantle of sands of the arena, spotted with purple, exalted herself in the light and believed herself to be a goddess. Young, dressed in the royal mourning of the black panthers, carrying, along her limbs intertwined so precisely, a few enormous scattered topazes, she darted the pure and fixed eye of those who have not yet contemplated, on the banks of the great desert rivers, their sinister pristine image. Her feline paws, powerful and childish in appearance, seemed to float over flakes of down. In three light leaps she reached the middle of the circus. There, sitting down, with a serious and undulating movement, any other business seeming to her of less importance, including the examination of the imperial box, she licked her sex.

Beside her, martyred Christians hung from tall crosses red with blood. A dead elephant barred with its gray mass, a colossal collapsed wall, a whole corner of the extraordinarily blue sky. In the distance, in circles of terraced steps, there was a mist of pale shapes from which came strange clamors, and the beast, having finished its intimate toilet, sought for a moment, muzzle to the ground, the reason for those cries of fury, inexplicable to her, whose cold and methodical morals only admitted the utility of murder without yet understanding its different hysteria. From them came the muffled roar of a windswept wave, complaints of branches cracking under the lightning. She let out a mocking mew that defied the storms, and, without hurrying too much, seized with the inconceivable caprice of showing them the gentleness of real ferocious beasts, she went to sit down in front of the tasty mass of the elephant, disdaining human prey. She drank at her leisure the steaming liquor dripping from the monstrous corpse, carved out a large shred of flesh, then, the feast over, sitting on the remains of her meal, she polished her left paw solicitously. Two days before her deliverance, they had sown, in the darkness of her prison, unworthy meats seasoned with cumin, sprinkled with saffron, to excite the devouring fire of her entrails; but the skillful scenter had abstained, having known longer fasts and more dangerous temptations. Not ignorant, although a virgin, she already knew the thirsts of the burning noon of her country, where the birds weep sad melodies while sighing after the rain. She knew the poisonous plants of the great inextricable forests, where forked-tongued reptiles distilled poison and tried to fascinate her. She knew the extreme size of certain suns, and the very ridiculous thinness of certain victims, the anxious waits under the evil eye of the moon which launches you treacherously in pursuit of an ever more and more fleeting shadow of game! From these unfortunate hunts, she had kept the instinct of a poor warrior, and only asked for a modest share so as not to feel dizzy in this other blessed world where the predators, who had become the brothers of man, seemed invited to solemn feasts. She chose her piece without boasting, desiring to prove well-bred in the presence of appetites less natural than hers.

A naked Christian, ridiculously armed with a whip with an iron ball, appeared above the rump of the elephant, pushed by executioners who could not be seen. He slipped in the clotted blood, rolled his forehead forward. Boos lifted him up. He picked up his whip again, and a smile tugged at his pale lips. He didn't want to use it, even against the beast that was going to cut his throat. He sat down, his pale eyes fixed on the enemy. The latter made the gesture of playing with her paw, a gesture signifying: "I am satisfied!" And she lay down, her eyes half-closed, waving her tail in perplexity. There was a tranquil duel of curious glances, the Christian seeking, despite the willed abandonment of his being, the secret of the tamers of wild beasts, the supreme power of the will alone over the brute, and the naked beast striving to disentangle the kind of power this species has when it is free.

A formidable clamor awoke them from their singular reverie. They were now the center of the bloody party, and no one really understood this way of having fun. A sudden anger invaded all the spectators. Beastmasters were called, horses galloped towards the elephant whose heavy mass was dragged away, and standing up, face to face, the two adversaries continued to watch each other. The Christian refused the fight, the panther did not feel the courage to slash, not being hungry anymore. One of the Beastmasters rushed forward, threatening them with his sword. With a graceful leap the animal avoided the strike, and the Christian kept his melancholy smile. Then screams rang out from all sides. The storm broke, terrible. The villains rushed against the beast, which declared itself, capriciously, for the weakest one. They went to lay the spears on the braziers, they brought the darts coated with pitch and burning feathers, they called the dogs trained to cut the shanks of the bulls, they filled vases with boiling oil. All hatred turned in a moment to the side where the mad girl, beating her sides with her indecisive tail, wondered what these preparations for war meant. The culprits did not give her time to come to her senses. They swooped down on her, and they were disorderly flyers in a track crowded with the dying. The panther fled, seized with a superstitious terror. This was the end of the world! Pell-mell, pursued and pursuers tumbled over the bodies of men and animals under the immense laughter of the people, whom this new buffoonery ended up relaxing. From all the places, stones, fruits, weapons were thrown at the distraught animal. Patricians threw jewels that hissed terribly through space, and the emperor, standing, stoned her himself with silver coins. With one last desperate leap, the panther, intoxicated with rage, bristling with arrows, surrounded by flames, took refuge in its cage, which remained open. The gate was closed again, and the dark trap descended back underground.

Days, nights flowed by, atrociously. From time to time she gave a lugubrious mew, a call to the sun that she was never to see again. Having become the legend of the circus, she was subjected to all the tortures. A coward, they said, she had refused the fight, and could no longer claim the rank of noble animal. The keeper of the beasts that were kept prisoners was a very old slave, without pity for that mouth which had been widened by the blade of a sword that she had bitten, only gave her the scraps of the neighboring cages, bones already gnawed, rotten, foul things, which were heaped up in her house as in a cesspool. His fur, soiled with filth, was covered with wounds. Young boys, to make fun, had nailed her tail to the ground until she had, with a painful effort, torn it from the nail, leaving some of her skin there. The old slave amused himself by defying her, offering her one hand while with the other he blinded her with a handful of sulfur. He completely burned an ear in the crackling fire of a torch. Deprived of air, of light, her mouth still filled with bloody drool, she was screaming miserably, looking for a way out, beating the bars with her skull, tearing the ground with her fingernails, and deep in her bowels a mysterious evil was born.

Because she growled too sinisterly, the order came to let her starve outright. Dignified deaths—strangulation or a stab in the heart—

were no longer for her. She was forgotten and the old watchman simply stopped walking past her with his torch. The beast understood. She grew silent, lay down in a last proud attitude, and, drawing around her her bruised tail, crossing her gangrenous paws, closing her fiery eyes, she dreamed while awaiting her agony. Oh! The forests that creak under the storm! The enormous suns, the moons the color of roses, the birds weeping for the rain, the greenery, the fresh springs, the easy young prey from which one can drink the life in a single aspiration, the great rivers spreading out their mirror where the leaning beasts have halos of stars... Gradually, the dying panther's brain was dazzled by ancient visions. Oh, happiness, far away, freedom! A movement of mad despair reminded her of her fate: she also saw again the golden field, stained with purple, the sand of the arenas, the gray mass of the disemboweled elephant, the harsh smile of the Christian, and finally the furious cries of the audience, the tortures, all the tortures! Her muzzle resting on her two fatally crossed legs, she seemed to be sleeping... perhaps she was already dead. Suddenly, the darkness of her prison dissipated. A trapdoor had just slid up, and, descending from the sky into this hell where the damned beast languished, a white, slender form, a woman, appeared. She carried a quarter of kid goat in the raised hem of her tunic, and on her shoulder her right arm supported a full vase. The panther stood up. This all-white creature was the daughter of the old keeper of the wild beasts:

"Beast," she said, while behind her swirled lights as blond as her hair, "I have compassion for you. You won't die."

Untying a chain, she pushed open the gate, dropped the quarter of kid on the threshold of the cage, gently set down the full vase with calm gestures.

Then the panther picked herself up on her loins, fortunately still supple, made herself very small so as not to frighten the child, watched her for a moment with her two phosphorescent eyes, which had become as deep as chasms, with a bound jumped at her throat and savaged her.

UNIVERSAL JOY

For Édouard Dubus

WHO is the fool or the madman who invented the idea of joyous nature?

From what herd of Panurge came those who reissued, at least a billion times a year, these childish clichés: *"the gaiety of the sun"*—*"the joy of spring"*—*"the joyful chatter of the birds"*—*"the immense feast of nature"*, etc., etc.? And because a gentleman had the idea of offering flowers to his mistress to congratulate her on being pretty, because the song of a caged canary entertains the cobbler of the corner, because in spring young men want to fondle girls, because the color of the sun is also that of gold, and gold represents all joys, the inhabitants of this land all believe in universal gaiety!

One day, we were slowly climbing a hill. It was a superb day, no clouds, no wind, neither too hot nor too cold, and the silence of high noon reigned.

My God, the terrible sadness that emanated from the landscape, *thinking about it a little more than usual.* How melancholy they fled, the distance drowned in a tender blue at first, and becoming almost black on the declines!

There was nobody. There was never anyone! The dark woods seemed unwilling secret things, determined not to reveal their mystery. Over our shoulder leaned an almond branch in bud, pink buds swollen like cold mouths. We thought that these distances, at first soft blue, then black on their decline, were still blue over there, would always be blue if we transported ourselves to the indefinite *over there*... always blue then successively black. And the dark woods have no other mystery to reveal to us than that of their very existence, a secret they keep despite the heavy numbers piled up. This branch of flowering almond tree, when it opens all its rosy mouths at once, will say nothing... nothing except what the passer-by poet will make it say.

Is nature therefore outside of us, when it is not spiritualized by us? I dare to find it impassible and sealed.

That day, we sadly descended the hill.

Who is the fool or the madman who invented the idea of joyous nature?

THE HANDS

For A.-Ferdinand Herold

OH! The obscene little hands, how I look at them with dread when I go out into society! In the air like an egret, like a flower of pink honeysuckle...

They go, they come, having no memory of the thing that they have done or that they will surely, irrevocably do.

They skip through the sugar cubes, they crumple the fan, they pout, they have tantrums, bursts of laughter, and, imperturbable, they put on their gloves to touch the foreign hand of the waltz partner, the hand of the unknown one, who might not be pure...

Oh! The obscene little hands over which we humbly lean, naive as we are, to lay down the respectful kiss of our admiration! Like little fat birds plucked raw, I suffocate with a desire to cry so much, they frighten me so, these obscene little hands!

A PARTIAL LIST OF SNUGGLY BOOKS

ETHEL ARCHER *The Hieroglyph*
ETHEL ARCHER *Phantasy and Other Poems*
ETHEL ARCHER *The Whirlpool*
G. ALBERT AURIER *Elsewhere and Other Stories*
CHARLES BARBARA *My Lunatic Asylum*
S. HENRY BERTHOUD *Misanthropic Tales*
LÉON BLOY *The Tarantulas' Parlor and Other Unkind Tales*
ÉLÉMIR BOURGES The Twilight of the Gods
CYRIEL BUYSSE *The Aunts*
KAREL ČAPEK *Krakatit*
JAMES CHAMPAGNE *Harlem Smoke*
FÉLICIEN CHAMPSAUR *The Latin Orgy*
BRENDAN CONNELL *Unofficial History of Pi Wei*
BRENDAN CONNELL (editor)
    The Zaffre Book of Occult Fiction
BRENDAN CONNELL (editor)
    The Zinzolin Book of Occult Fiction
RAFAELA CONTRERAS *The Turquoise Ring and Other Stories*
ADOLFO COUVE *When I Think of My Missing Head*
RENÉ CREVEL *Are You All Crazy?*
QUENTIN S. CRISP *Aiaigasa*
QUENTIN S. CRISP *Graves*
LUCIE DELARUE-MARDRUS *The Last Siren and Other Stories*
LADY DILKE *The Outcast Spirit and Other Stories*
ÉDOUARD DUJARDIN *Hauntings*
BERIT ELLINGSEN *Now We Can See the Moon*
ERCKMANN-CHATRIAN *A Malediction*
ALPHONSE ESQUIROS *The Enchanted Castle*
ENRIQUE GÓMEZ CARRILLO *Sentimental Stories*
DELPHI FABRICE *Flowers of Ether*
DELPHI FABRICE *The Red Sorcerer*
DELPHI FABRICE *The Red Spider*
BENJAMIN GASTINEAU *The Reign of Satan*
EDMOND AND JULES DE GONCOURT *Manette Salomon*
REMY DE GOURMONT *From a Faraway Land*
REMY DE GOURMONT *Morose Vignettes*
GUIDO GOZZANO *Alcina and Other Stories*
GUSTAVE GUICHES *The Modesty of Sodom*
EDWARD HERON-ALLEN *The Complete Shorter Fiction*
EDWARD HERON-ALLEN *Three Ghost-Written Novels*

J.-K. HUYSMANS *The Crowds of Lourdes*
COLIN INSOLE *Valerie and Other Stories*
JUSTIN ISIS *Pleasant Tales II*
JULES JANIN *The Dead Donkey and the Guillotined Woman*
KLABUND *Spook*
GUSTAVE KAHN *The Mad King*
KLABUND *Spook*
MARIE KRYSINSKA *The Path of Amour*
BERNARD LAZARE *The Mirror of Legends*
BERNARD LAZARE *The Torch-Bearers*
JULES LERMINA *Human Life*
MAURICE LEVEL *The Shadow*
JEAN LORRAIN *Errant Vice*
JEAN LORRAIN *Masks in the Tapestry*
GEORGES DE LYS *An Idyll in Sodom*
GEORGES DE LYS *Penthesilea*
ARTHUR MACHEN *Ornaments in Jade*
PAUL MARGUERITTE *Pantomimes and Other Surreal Tales*
CAMILLE MAUCLAIR *The Frail Soul and Other Stories*
CATULLE MENDÈS *Mephistophela*
ÉPHRAÏM MIKHAËL *Halyartes and Other Poems in Prose*
LUIS DE MIRANDA *Who Killed the Poet?*
OCTAVE MIRBEAU *The 628-E8*
CHARLES MORICE *Babels, Balloons and Innocent Eyes*
GABRIEL MOUREY *Monada*
DAMIAN MURPHY *Daughters of Apostasy*
KRISTINE ONG MUSLIM *Butterfly Dream*
OSSIT *Ilse*
CHARLES NODIER *Jean Sbogar and Other Stories*
CHARLES NODIER *Outlaws and Sorrows*
HERSH DOVID NOMBERG *A Cheerful Soul and Other Stories*
PHILOTHÉE O'NEDDY *The Enchanted Ring*
GEORGES DE PEYREBRUNE *A Decadent Woman*
HÉLÈNE PICARD *Sabbat*
JEAN PRINTEMPS *Whimsical Tales*
RACHILDE *The Blood-Guzzler and Other Stories*
RACHILDE *The Princess of Darkness*
JEREMY REED *When a Girl Loves a Girl*
ADOLPHE RETTÉ *Misty Thule*
JEAN RICHEPIN *The Bull-Man and the Grasshopper*
FREDERICK ROLFE (Baron Corvo) *Amico di Sandro*
JASON ROLFE *An Archive of Human Nonsense*

ARNAUD RYKNER *The Last Train*
ROBERT SCHEFFER *Prince Narcissus and Other Stories*
ROBERT SCHEFFER *The Green Fly and Other Stories*
MARCEL SCHWOB *The Assassins and Other Stories*
MARCEL SCHWOB *Double Heart*
CHRISTIAN HEINRICH SPIESS *The Dwarf of Westerbourg*
BRIAN STABLEFORD (editor) *The Snuggly Satyricon*
BRIAN STABLEFORD (editor) *The Snuggly Satanicon*
BRIAN STABLEFORD *Spirits of the Vasty Deep*
COUNT ERIC STENBOCK *The Shadow of Death*
COUNT ERIC STENBOCK *Studies of Death*
MONTAGUE SUMMERS *The Bride of Christ and Other Fictions*
MONTAGUE SUMMERS *Six Ghost Stories*
ALICE TÉLOT *The Inn of Tears*
GILBERT-AUGUSTIN THIERRY *Reincarnation and Redemption*
DOUGLAS THOMPSON *The Fallen West*
TOADHOUSE *Gone Fishing with Samy Rosenstock*
TOADHOUSE *Living and Dying in a Mind Field*
TOADHOUSE *What Makes the Wave Break?*
LÉO TRÉZENIK *The Confession of a Madman*
LÉO TRÉZENIK *Decadent Prose Pieces*
RUGGERO VASARI *Raun*
ILARIE VORONCA *The Confession of a False Soul*
ILARIE VORONCA *The Key to Reality*
JANE DE LA VAUDÈRE *The Demi-Sexes and The Androgynes*
JANE DE LA VAUDÈRE
The Double Star and Other Occult Fantasies
JANE DE LA VAUDÈRE
The Mystery of Kama and Brahma's Courtesans
JANE DE LA VAUDÈRE
Three Flowers and The King of Siam's Amazon
JANE DE LA VAUDÈRE
The Witch of Ecbatana and The Virgin of Israel
AUGUSTE VILLIERS DE L'ISLE-ADAM *Isis*
RENÉE VIVIEN *Lilith's Legacy*
RENÉE VIVIEN *A Woman Appeared to Me*
ILARIE VORONCA *The Confession of a False Soul*
ILARIE VORONCA *The Key to Reality*
TERESA WILMS MONTT *In the Stillness of Marble*
TERESA WILMS MONTT *Sentimental Doubts*
KAREL VAN DE WOESTIJNE *The Dying Peasant*